BERKELEY, May 15, 1969 — Riot police carrying shotguns killed one bystander and wounded several protestors. When interviewed at the hospital, one protestor observed, "getting shot in the ass has certain strategic connotations. One, it suggests that you have pissed somebody off. Two, that you are running away from that somebody. And three, that somebody has got the guns and you don't." All of those things were true at People's Park on Bloody Thursday.

Nursing rage, disappointment and a sore behind, young Gus Bessemer heads for the Colorado Rockies to get away from it all, only to discover that — even surrounded by rugged mountain beauty — there's no escaping the war at home . . . or himself.

Praise for *A Bowl Full of Nails*

"In the final analysis, *A Bowl Full of Nails* explores the possibility that our battles with the world around us may often be manifestations of our own, innermost struggles."

— Delin Colón, author of *Rasputin and The Jews: A Reversal of History*

"*A Bowl Full of Nails* offers the reader an amazing story, well told, with evocative powers of description that take your breath away. Degelman has a marvelous way of building suspense that lures the reader on a trip into the past, to a power place where big things happened. I could taste the '60s gestalt in the back of my throat."

— Destiny Kinal, author of *Burning Silk*

"In *A Bowl Full of Nails*, the author reminds us that the '60s weren't just about flowers and stoned hippies. With a dynamic plot that keeps you on the edge of your seat, this rough-edged tale bursts with humor, tragedy, betrayal, espionage, clueless communards, anarchist maniacs, and murderous agents provocateur. If you ever thought you could get away by running from the big city, Degelman has news for you."

— Mary Mackey, author of *Season of Shadows*

A BOWL FULL OF NAILS

A novel

Charles Degelman

Harvard Square Editions
www.harvardsquareeditions.org
New York
2014

Publisher's Note: This is a work of fiction. Names, characters,
places, and incidents are a product of the author's imagination.
Locales and public names are sometimes used for atmospheric
purposes. Any resemblance to actual people, living or dead, or
to businesses, companies, events, institutions, or locales is
completely coincidental.

Published in the United States by Harvard Square Editions
www.harvardsquareeditions.org
A Bowl Full of Nails Charles Degelman
ISBN 978-0-9895960-4-6
Printed in the United States of America

Front cover drawing © Bill Young
Back cover photo © Alexey Sergeev

For those who dare swim upstream

Still here I carry my old delicious burdens . . .

    —Walt Whitman, *Song of the Open Road*

BLOODY THURSDAY

"Don't come over here."

I'd never heard Super Joel whisper before.

"It's the Meanies," he hissed into the phone. "They're packin' shotguns."

"Blue Meanies with heat?" *Nothing new there*, I thought. The Blue Meanies were Alameda County Sheriff deputies trained to fight the war at home. We named them after the cartoon juggernauts who pursued the Beatles in that ridiculous movie about a yellow submarine. "I mean . . . nobody's been shot," I said. "Right?"

"No," Super Joel said. "Not yet."

"Well, there ya go!"

The Blue Meanies wore powder-blue coveralls with service pistols, gas masks, and other military-issue crap slung beneath their beer bellies. The blue coveralls hid badges, making it difficult to link any one Meanie to any particular act of violence.

"I don't know, man," Super Joel whispered. "This is different."

"What do you mean 'different'?"

"Like, different, man. Like a bad moon rising, okay?" Super Joel sounded like a hippie, but he wasn't. Super Joel was a hard-headed agitator and a full-blown anarchist who didn't let anybody stop him . . . from anything.

"I don't like it," Joel continued. "The scene today. It's not gonna be, like, manageable."

"How come you're whispering?"

"I'm whispering?"

"You're whispering," I said. "Shit, Joel, I never heard you do anything but holler before."

"Okay, smart ass," he growled. "Bring your goddam show over here. Try to get your truck up to People's Park and put on a show. You'll see how funny it is."

Click.

Dial tone.

People's Park began as a hangout. Hatched in a vacant lot owned by the University of California, the project mushroomed. Soon an amorphous cohort of Berkeley street people were planting vegetable gardens, trees, and roll-out sod. They liberated benches, chairs, old couches and hammocks and arranged them in convivial powwow circles.

Flags and tie-dyed banners, political slogans and silk-screened portraits of Che Guevara hung in festoons from poles rigged with cabaret lights. Rebel electricians had bootlegged juice off the city power grid. As soon as the city cut the connection, the electricians rewired it a different way.

A motley crowd hung out in the park — lovers and hustlers, street musicians, suburban kids looking for action. Groups of hippies and other freaks gathered to smoke and deal dope and a line of conga drummers rumbled infectiously. A free store swapped out clothes for furniture, tents for books and paintings. University grad students and professors conducted teach-ins on everything from the history of Indochina to civil disobedience and composting. Knowledge, baby, is power.

So, on that Bloody Thursday, our People's Theater Collective humped across the San Francisco Bay Bridge aboard a flatbed truck full of theater weaponry: a puppet stage, a bass drum, a dinged and dented tuba, and a battery of stage drops, flags, and banners. After the truck burst out of the San Francisco fog into the Berkeley sunshine, we almost made it to Telegraph Avenue before a handful of shotgun-wielding Meanies closed in around the truck.

"Good morning, officers." Benny was driving. Benny was a tough, stubby little thespian from working-class

Baltimore who had abandoned a "diamond in the rough" scholarship at Harvard to join the revolution.

"Where you going with this load of crap?" The chief Meanie jerked his head toward the back of the truck — and at me.

"Well, sir," Benny replied, "we were invited to do a performance on Sproul Plaza. I believe you'll find we have a permit on file at the Chancellor's Office."

This was bullshit. The UC administration would have given itself an enema before they granted a permit allowing the People's Theater Collective to rouse the rabble on campus.

The Meanie wasn't about to check with anybody. "Turn this shit heap around and get the hell out of here!"

A cluster of bigger, badder Meanies closed in around the truck.

"Just do what the Man says," I whispered into the cab. Funny. I was whispering just like Super Joel.

"Yessir, sir!" Benny saluted the head Meanie, ground the truck into reverse, hung a Y-turn into a driveway, and headed us back the way we came.

I shivered as we drove past the prickly cluster of shotguns, barrels crazy-aimed everywhere — at the blue sky, the Berkeley street, between my shoulder blades. I leaned over the cab as Benny headed South on Sacramento Avenue. "Nice work, Benny. You sounded so sweet."

"Thanks, man. Well, those guys are my brothers, aren't they? Just because they kicked the shit out of us last week."

I had straightened up and relaxed my shoulders when Benny yanked a right onto a side street. The tuba tumbled out of its perch and slammed against the side rail of the truck, picking up another dent in its soft coils. "What are you doing?" I shouted over the wind while I righted the collapsed puppet stage.

"Fuck them," Benny said. "We came to do a show."

"Fuck them," I repeated to myself. *So we were driving behind enemy lines. No big deal, right?*

"I'm just gonna head up and around and come in on the North side of the campus. There won't be so much action up . . ."

"Blam! Blam-blam!"

Benny slammed on the brakes. Gunshots weren't surprising. Cops launched teargas canisters all the time but on Bloody Thursday, these detonations didn't carry the dull "thud" of teargas cartridges. Something was — as Super Joel said — different. Bad moon rising.

A retreating army of students, hippies, and bystanders stampeded toward us, faces full of fear. There was none of the hysterical laughter, shrieks, and epithets that usually accompanied a rout by the pigs. These kids weren't laughing, they weren't shouting, and they weren't looking back. They were running.

Further up towards Telegraph Avenue and the Park, Blue Meanies had broken ranks. Every so often, one of them would stop long enough to raise his gun and fire. I saw a studenty-looking girl scream and spin, swatting at her back and arms. She looked like she'd been bitten by angry bees. Her knees buckled and she fell to the ground.

The crowd hit us.

"Get out! Get out!" A kid shouted through a bandana twisted across his face. "They got live ammo!" He sounded like a surprised child.

The fleeing demonstrators streamed around us. Others scuttled down the sidewalk behind the parked cars, keeping low, running crablike down the quaint blocks that sheltered the academics of Berkeley, California. Benny and I and the rest of the thespians abandoned ship and ran with the others.

"Shit," Benny hollered. "I left the keys in the truck."

I ran back, yanked open the truck door, and grabbed the keys. A rattle of pellets hit the truck. A slashing pain roared up my spinal column like I'd been doused in boiling water. I tried to turn and run but nothing happened. My butt, back, and legs went numb and I felt myself slipping down, down, past the running board, onto the pavement, into the broken-cigarette, popsicle-stick, candy-wrapper detritus of the street. I went all white and woozy, like I needed sleep.

BREAKFAST NAILS

Tink . . .

Tink . . .

I lay face down on the Indian print spread that covered the couch, ass in the air, while my girlfriend, Katie, tweezed birdshot pellets out of my butt cheeks. Now, getting shot in the ass has certain strategic connotations. One, it suggests that you have pissed somebody off. Two, that you are running away from that somebody. And three, that somebody has got the guns and you don't. All of those things were true in Berkeley California on Bloody Thursday, May 8, 1969.

"Ouch!"

Between stinging birdshot extractions, I made my rebuttal. We were guerrilla warriors, modeling ourselves after the Viet Cong and Ho Chi Minh and General Giap, the political and military genius who directed the fight for independence that the Vietnamese called simply "The

American War." But here, in the war at home, we lacked the discipline, experience, guerrilla tactics, and political profundity of the Vietcong. Besides, we didn't have guns and wouldn't have used them if we did. Our only weapon was rage at injustice, our belief in protest, and a wild, anarchic energy. Sure, the forces of good will prevail in the long run but on Bloody Thursday the battle wasn't equal and I wasn't taking that in, despite my pellet-riddled *derrière*.

"How long before they get tired of this game?" Katie swabbed alcohol on the little black scabs that had formed on my back, butt, and legs.

"What game?" I winced.

Birdshot penetrates the flesh to varying levels. The emergency room doctor had gotten to most of the pellets but he warned me that others might surface.

"Youch!" I hollered, as tweezers probed my flesh.

"You ready to take to the hills, cowpoke?" Katie asked.

"What are you talking about?"

"You came home after they let you out of the hospital." She dug again.

"Youch!" I squirmed in pain. "Yeah? So?"

"So. You think they'd have let you go if this was for real?"

"It's for real. They don't know what we're gonna do next."

"They have you on file. Your prints, a mug shot."

"That's nothing new."

"Yeah, Gus, there's plenty that's new."

"What?"

"You're on the list for Santa Rita."

"No shit," I said proudly.

Santa Rita was an old prison camp the county was renovating to use as a holding facility for overzealous Bay Area activists. The Berkeley Barb, the San Francisco Chronicle, the Oakland Tribune had hollered bloody murder, comparing Santa Rita to an American Auschwitz. The potential was there.

"So finally," Katie continued. "When do they decide to round up the people on that list? You, me? The kids? What do we do with the kids if we get busted? Ever think of that, Mister Ho Chi Minh?" One more sharp, stinging jolt and I heard another pellet land in the saucer.

I looked over. It was smeared with blood.

"Speak of the devil," Katie said.

Nine-year-old Amelia loped through the front door headed straight for the refrigerator. I got up and stumbled into the bathroom holding my pants away from my stinging rear end.

Cody came in to piss with me. "Red cross," he said, his tiny, clear stream intersecting mine.

"Get out of your school clothes before you go outside," I told him. Cody could bust through a pair of jeans quicker than a pipefitter. He took off into the back garden, exploding with after-school energy.

When I wasn't doing free shows in the parks of San Francisco, I lived across the Bay with Katie and her two kids in a flowery low-rent bungalow perched on a brown hillside above the sprawling city of Richmond, California. Below the bungalow, a petroleum refinery chuffed like a mechanical dragon. Oily mist hung in the air, smelling sickly-sweet from the effluvia of long-dead fossils. Flares from the refinery's burn-off towers and cracking plants, trapped and reflected by the summer-long ceiling of bay fog, made the whole world pulsate with a wild, orange light.

The refinery created a bizarre industrial counterpoint to the ramshackle comfort of the bungalow with its rose garden and sunny kitchen. We took a grim satisfaction, Katie and I, from sitting above the stinking jumble of towers, tanks, and pipelines while the refinery pounded out its toxic-industrial mantra. It was like living on top of an apocalypse.

On winter nights I descended to the leaky garage built into the hillside below the bungalow to build a redwood camper shell for the back of my truck. Beneath the dim light of a single overhead bulb, I cut, chiseled, screwed and glued white pine struts together. I ripped the resawn redwood ply to size and screwed it to the struts, all the time surrounded by fragrant pine shavings and rust-red sawdust. For reasons unknown to me then, I was recollecting the skills my father had given me.

When I was nine, I had built a soap box racer with my old man in the basement of our Massachusetts home. This was no jalopy. This was a bona fide racing machine, constructed according to the specs and blueprints of the National Soap Box Derby, held annually in Akron, Ohio, Tire Capital of the World or so it was called in 1954, when the ore belt was still high on the momentum of World War Two, knocking out cars as quick as they could haul coal, steel, and rubber to Detroit.

Night after night, the racer took shape under the warm cone of light that separated the workbench from the dank recesses of the coal bin and the furnace room. My old man taught me how to guide a bucking, kicking saber saw along a pattern scribed onto a sheet of three-quarter-inch plywood. I learned how to mix water with the fine powder of composite resin glue and spread the stuff evenly over the pine frame members before I screwed down the masonite skin with a big, well-oiled Yankee screwdriver. I learned how to push a brace and bit against my chest while I drilled clearance holes for the carriage bolts that would clamp the axle, sandwiched between two two-by-fours, to the floorboards.

Before we shut out the light each night, my old man and I would stand back and admire our progress. The scent of plywood and pine pitch, vaporized by the friction of drill bits, saw blades, and sandpaper, merged with the fishy odor of the glue pot and the molasses sweetness of my old man's

Pall Malls. Now, as I built the camper, I began to realize that the reactivation of my carpentry skills was a sad, sweet attempt to reunite with my old man's spirit. I had just completed building the camper when I got shot in the butt on Bloody Thursday.

Now, in the kitchen I heard the klink of a knife in a peanut butter jar. Katie was talking to Amelia about school. In contrast to her tone with me, Katie's voice sounded light, happy, relieved to be with her daughter, grateful for the peace they shared.

I stumbled back to the couch, holding my pants up around my buttocks.

"How's your butt, Gus?" Amelia stood in the doorway beside Katie. At seven she already had her mother's reedy limbs and frame.

"It hurts. But pretty soon I'll be jumping around like Howdy Doody."

"Howdy Doody's a puppet," Amelia said, and headed for the bedroom balancing a treat of bread and peanut butter on each open palm.

"The harder you push," Katie said, "the harder they push back. You go back to Berkeley loaded for bear, they'll call in the National Guard. Or the Air Force." She followed the kids into the bedroom. "Moron," she mumbled over her shoulder.

I watched her settle onto the lower tier of the bunk bed, helping her little boy tie his sneakers.

"Last year, after Tet," I hollered from the couch, "Westmoreland begs for half a million more teenagers to kill. What did Johnson say?"

"Who cares? He was the President. He was bound to say something stupid."

"Johnson said, 'If I give you half a million more young Americans men, Herr General, I cannot guarantee our national security here at home.' National security! He was talking about us, that's who. We're the threat to national security. Us, the Mobilization, the Panthers, the whole mess of hell no, free-city outlaws . . ."

Katie stopped me in mid-rant. "You can't think of anything but getting back at these bozos: the Generals, big fat President Johnson and all those other half-dead, white guys. They're not your father. Leave them alone. Before they kill you. Before they kill all of us. They stink and it's beginning to smell in here, too." Katie disappeared into the sunlit backyard to join her kids.

I pulled up my pants and followed her into the yard. There, squinting into the sunshine, surrounded by the reds and oranges and lavenders of roses, geraniums, and daisies, Cody and Amelia watched wide-eyed while I hollered.

The next morning, Katie served me a bowl full of nails. The kids laughed while I faked eating with gusto. I looked up. Katie wasn't laughing.

"Thanks, Mom." I pushed the bowl away, rose from the table and left the house. I got it. Katie was clear and so was I. My neighbor, Dave West, carpenter extraordinaire, had recently told me about a job to be had, working as a handyman for an old lady who lived high in the Colorado Rockies. I walked up to Dave's place. The job was still open.

"I need to spend time alone," I explained to Katie on my return. "Work with my hands. Get close to nature."

Katie listened from the kitchen door, arms folded beneath her breasts. "What about the theater company?"

"They'll get along without me," I said. "Where one tree falls, a thousand will take its place."

"Great. Quotations from Chairman Mao."

"Ho Chi Minh."

" 'Where one tree falls,' " she repeated. "Shit, man, you haven't fallen anywhere. You're just running away from yourself."

"I don't need your advice," I hissed. "I'm gonna get my head together, that's all. Now leave me alone."

"With pleasure." She kicked away from the doorjamb.

I gathered up my clothes, a few books, my guitar, and my carpentry tools and — still smarting from the birdshot — packed them into my truck with the new, redwood camper I had built on the back of my '56 Chevy pickup.

"You better take Wooly and Zoom with you," Cody said. "Then you won't be all alone."

"Yeah, you better," Amelia agreed.

"Just as well," Katie added. "I'm off with the kids to Grandma's and you weren't planning to come anyway, were you?"

I nodded, my eyes full of tears. I hadn't remembered Katie's plans for the summer, hadn't considered the kids, the dogs, any of it. All was lost in the hurricane of my revolutionary fervor. I was grateful for the kids' suggestion. Wooly and Zoom would provide a link to whatever the hell I was about to leave.

Canines and Porcupines

I woke to the approaching whine of truck tires. There was no light in the bathroom for the kids. Katie was nowhere to be seen, felt, or smelt. Headlights backlit the canvas flap at the rear of my redwood camper. Wooly and Zoom whined and shifted uncomfortably. Slowly, my eyes dilated in the darkness. Sprawled in the back of my pickup, I lay tangled in my sleeping bag, still in greasy dungarees. The sweat on my socks had turned frigid and the blood from a skinned knuckle had coagulated in the cold night air. The unpainted redwood walls of the camper closed in around me.

The semi blew past, its turbulence rocking the pickup. Cattle trucks had been keeping me company since I had come off the Eastern slope of the Sierras the night before.

"Come on guys," I growled at the dogs. I put my feet on the cold steel of the pickup bed. "Take a leak. I'll get coffee'd up, you can munch down your kibbles and we'll hit the road."

Wooly and Zoom tumbled onto the roadside apron.

I pulled on my boots and stepped outside.

Morning comes quickly to the desert. A gash of red showed on the eastern horizon. I set up my tiny stove and watched the pressurized flame of the burner lick blue and yellow around the coffee pot. This was what I wanted, wasn't it? Getting away from it all? Heading for the simple life? I'd had enough bird shot, tear gas, and frustration to last me a lifetime. I'd also had enough of Katie's disapproval. I would live out of time, beyond urgency. My ass would heal; my head would clear. I would keep my own company, stand on my own two feet, fart out loud, sleep with a million chicks, and realize my own destiny.

Yeah, right.

I threw a handful of coffee into the boiling water and gave a holler for Wooly and Zoom. My heart began to pound. Wise, young Cody had been right. The dogs had already become my lifeline to a fast-disappearing past.

The sunrise expanded into clear, bright daylight. I couldn't see either animal on the hardscrabble and scrub landscape that stretched away from the truck. I pulled out their bag of kibbles, banged together a couple of pie tins. "Wooly! Zoom!" My voice sounded puny in the void.

Nothing.

Another cattle truck blasted past, heading east. I could hear the doomed animals bawling inside. To market, to market, jiggety jig. The whining tires receded, leaving me with the desert, my Chevy, and no dogs.

I grabbed my binoculars out of the tool compartment and climbed onto the camper to get a better view. Wooly, short for Wooly Bully, was named by Cody from the tune by Sam the Shan and the Pharaohs. Wooly was a big, handsome malamute mutt. You could see him a mile away. Zoom was a black and brown, two-tone, shoeshine-colored Labrador. He could easily blend into the background, but he didn't usually stray far from Wooly.

I scanned the sagebrush. Sandstone pinks and purples rushed across the binocular lenses. I had been a fool to let them run off. I heard barking carried on the breeze. I pounded the pie tins again and called out their names. What was out there that could hold them? Below, the coffee boiled out of the pot and onto the burner. The flame hissed out.

The sun rose hot and high. Sporadic traffic magnified the silence of the lake bed as each traveler streamed into view and roared past to disappear over the horizon. There was nothing to do but wait.

I pulled a quart can of paint and a brush out of my tool box and painted a red star on each door of my '56 Chevy pickup. No dogs. I poured a puddle of the red paint on the tarmac, pushed my palm into the hot color and branded each front fender. I knew the Lakota Sioux had placed handprints on the flanks of their horses to signal a coup on an enemy. Despite my birdshot butt, I had counted coup on my own adversaries. Alone on the road, my dogs gone missing, I would form a one-man Red army, red star, Lakota hand and all. *You're out of your mind,* I told myself. *You just raised a shiny red flag for every state trooper and sheriff from here to Colorado.* Still, my red-paint signification kept my mind focused in the wilderness of roadside trash, barbed-wire fences, sage and tumbleweed and the hands looked totally cool on the dark green flanks of my pickup.

The sun roared toward its zenith, the temperature rose, and I was running low on drinking water. Here they came, loping down the highway, Zoom in the lead. My shoulders sagged with relief. Now we could get on with it. By nightfall I would be outside of Salt Lake City and in another day I would be safe in my Rocky mountain hermitage.

Thirty yards out, I realized that Zoom had gotten into something. White froth foamed at his mouth. Both hounds were moving easily enough but their noses, forelegs, and paws were full of small, white-and-black lances. They approached the truck and sat on their haunches, panting saliva. Porcupines. My dogs — our dogs — were dripping blood in tiny beads around each quill. And yet they seemed cheerful, as if they had been on a great adventure and wanted to tell me about it.

I grabbed Zoom and put him between my legs. An 18-wheeler roared by, air horn bellowing. I put my fingers around a quill and tugged. It didn't budge. I looked closely at his snout. Tiny barbs on each quill made them impossible to pull. Panicked, I shoved both the dogs into the back of the truck. I had no idea what to do. How seriously were they injured? Were the quills poisonous? Infectious? One day out and I had fucked up already.

Wooly hopped up onto my sleeping bag, panting, the pain beginning to set into his thick doggie skull. I stomped around to the highway side of the truck, opened the compartment, pulled out a pair of pliers and prepared to operate. By now, both dogs had quieted down. The poor creatures couldn't put their heads down; their chins were prickled with quills. I tried the pliers. I got a few out, but it was impossible to keep the dogs from struggling.

Finding a vet would mean heading into the nearest town. No good. I was driving the back roads because I wanted to avoid the law. Katie wasn't the only person I had pissed off. There were subpoenas out for me — and hundreds like me — for inciting to riot at People's Park, meaning we were wanted for getting within birdshot range of the Blue Meanies. That was back in California. I was in Nevada. Were they in touch? How effectively? I didn't know.

I poked my head inside the canvas flap. Wooly and Zoom looked up at me with sad eyes. Both dogs were drooling from the quills. Subpoenas, warrants, whatever. Fuck it. Notorious or anonymous, I had to do something. Fast. According to the map, Tonopah was the closest town. I turned to the dogs and shouted through the camper window. "I hope you two motherfuckers got something to eat off that porcupine, 'cause until we find a vet, your chomping privileges are over."

Neither dog had the heart to talk back.

Tonopah, Nevada had been blasted out of hell. On the outskirts of town, a phalanx of rusted-out road graders, bulldozers, and dump trucks sat abandoned to the elements behind a sagging chain-link fence. A cinderblock bodega squatted next to the windowless cube of the Galaxy Club. Strictly utility drinking. The parking lot was empty except for two dusty pickups and a flatbed. It was too hot to be out in the noonday sun, even for desert rats.

I filled the dog's bowls with water and tethered them to the inside of the camper. They looked miserable.

I slouched into the cool, dark bunker and ordered a beer from the silent bartender. Not a nod or greeting from the melancholics who inhabited the stools. After buying a round of beers, the bartender opened up. A vet lived up there, out on the mesa. All I had to do was head out east on Road 14, take a left on Snake Canyon Road — it didn't have no sign but it was the third turnoff north of the dry wash. If I got to the flood channel down there I had gone too far.

Blinded by the light outside, I bade farewell to the charms of the Galaxy Club, checked the Misery Twins in the back of the truck, and followed the sparse directions up a long, straight road. It climbed like a pencil line up a desert slope to a series of switchbacks that traversed the steep walls of the mesa. The bartender might have been stingy with his words, but he had directed me straight. We pulled into the rutted yard of a one-story whitewashed adobe with a green cross painted on the wall. Cottonwoods shaded a mud-splattered Ford Bronco that had seen more desert dirt than pavement. I quieted the dogs and walked up the pathway to the porch. The door was open and the inside beckoned, dark and cool.

A tall man sat behind a desk, austere, wire-rimmed glasses perched on a crowlike beak, a white linen shirt buttoned up to his Adam's apple. He looked like a Kansas preacher. An open window behind the desk looked beyond the shade thrown by the cottonwoods. Merciless sunlight baked the open land and a row of gray-blue hills shimmered in the distance.

"My dogs got into trouble with a porcupine," I said.

"Happens all the time out here." He rose and stretched, never taking his eyes off me.

I brought the dogs in. They stood, panting and dripping blood, heads hung low with fatigue and doggy guilt.

He cleared the remains of a breakfast off a stainless steel operating table. His arms and legs moved like stovepipes set at awkward angles in his body. "I'm gonna have to put 'em out," he told me. While he was shooting my dogs full of anesthesia, he glanced up, eyes drilling right through mine, as if he'd opened a door to my skull.

He set to work on Wooly, pulling bloodstained, ivory-colored javelins with a pair of surgical pliers. After he dropped each quill into a stainless steel pan, his eyes would return to mine. Unlike the pellets the doctors and Katie had pulled out of my own carcass, the quills did not go "tink." The process did strike me as parallel studies in foolishness, however, and I wondered how Katie must have felt as I groaned beneath her ministrations.

The way this vet glanced at me, I wondered if he'd seen my picture on a wanted poster. The bulletin boards of post offices were plastered with mug shots of kids wanted by the FBI. Photos of long-haired boys and girls dragged off a college campus kept company with the grizzled, hard-eyed criminals of my childhood. The board with the booking numbers hung beneath glasses and shaggy locks, over plaid shirts, turtlenecks, navy pea jackets, and army fatigues. Young eyes flashed with defiance — shame had no place in these portraits.

Another quill plunked into the basin. Wooly sighed in his sleep.

"We're gettin' our asses kicked over there, ain't we?" the veterinarian said.

I didn't know what he was getting at, and I didn't want to talk about anything but the weather for at least another thousand miles. I shrugged my shoulders and kept mum.

"Tee-vee don't say much but you can tell. The way they talk about it. Try to cover it up with the score, like it was a ball game. So many killed this week, so many wounded. Body counts. That ain't no way to win a war. Now you and me . . ." He swabbed Wooly's bloody head with a cloth. "We know better. Ain't no winners in wartime. Am I right?" He picked up Wooly and put him in my arms. "They say you fellas oughta be ashamed, not beatin' them Vietnamese Communists." He snorted and went to work on Zoom. "Communists? Shit, they look more like farmers to me." The vet fell quiet except for the sounds of exertion as he pulled quills from Zoom's snout, paws, and throat. "I landed at Salerno back in '43."

This guy thought I was a Vietnam vet. How could that be? I didn't wear a fatigue jacket or those military issue jungle boots with the green mesh insteps. What was the confusion?

When he finished, he lifted Zoom off the table and we both headed out the door, lugging the still-drugged hounds to my truck.

"Thanks for your help," I said, changing the subject. "I would have been sunk without you." I gave the man my last $20. "That's about all I got, except for gas money," I said.

He gave it back to me.

I thrust the money back at him. I didn't want to risk the chance of getting into a hollering match about draft dodgers or peace-loving cowards, but I was damned if I would take advantage of his services under false pretenses.

"Suit yourself," he said, pocketing the $20. "You keep headin' east, boy."

I thanked him and took off with my somnambulant canine load, heading east, away from the war in Vietnam, away from the war at home, away from my life and whatever phantom this guy saw inside of me.

MONTGOMERY, COLORADO

The canyons deepened, the hillsides steepened and spikes of Douglas fir began to climb the ragged ridges around us. Periodically the canyon walls would fall away to reveal green mountain meadows. Beyond them, miles-high blocks of frosted granite reared into the air.

"I hope this is what it's gonna be like. I hope this is what it's gonna be like," I chanted to the dogs while we dragged up the grade in third gear, the Chevy carburetor gasping for breath in the thinning air.

Snouts healing, the dogs kept a quiet watch out the back as the road unwound behind the pickup. I rounded a rocky bend cut into the hillside and there it was —

MONTGOMERY, CO
ELEVATION 9253 FEET
POP: 70

Bullet holes pockmarked the green sign and a proud parent had lined out the "~~70~~" and written "71."

I stopped the truck and looked down on the town nestled in the canyon below. One side was bathed in sunlight while the other side waited to be lit. A jumble of ramshackle huts, log cabins, and asbestos-shingled cottages clung to both sides of the ravine, defying gravity and the elements.

Above the cabins, abandoned mine portals spewed sand and gravel downhill from the ridgeline. A gaunt, iron head frame clawed toward the brilliant sky, signaling the opening of a mine shaft. Dave West, the guy who hipped me to this job had said that Montgomery was a mining town. That was an understatement. The original inhabitants had built the town around the mines.

A gravel road snaked down the hill between a row of abandoned stores and a rust-colored warehouse. The behemoth resembled a great iron ship and dominated Montgomery's main street. Across the road, a scabby old gas pump stood like a lone sentinel guarding a white clapboard storefront. The road followed a creek past more cabins on the sunny side of the canyon and disappeared into the dark pines below. Nothing stirred. The whole town appeared to have been cast aside, abandoned by the fickle undulations in the price of gold.

I stopped between the storefronts and the rusty warehouse. The big building was sheathed entirely in corrugated tin, from its massive stone foundation to the steep-pitched roof three stories above. Over a weathered, iron-strapped door, a faded sign proclaimed International Order of Odd Fellows, established in 1887. Odd fellows? Hell, the whole damned town was odd. A breeze wafted down the canyon, rippling the aspens. The Odd Fellows' Hall creaked and shifted like an ancient mariner, a witness to the boom and bust of this odd village.

As I began my descent through the village, a woman in a long skirt stepped out of a cabin and tossed a dishpan of water into a bed of growing things. She cradled the dishpan on her hip and waved.

I waved back, relieved at the first sign of life.

A light blue International truck glided past, engine silent. The driver had no shirt. A black beard and a pony tail hung symmetrically down the front and back of his naked torso. Once past me, the driver dropped the clutch, the engine caught, and he was away down the canyon.

"Come on, boys." I gave each dog a pat on his bony skull and followed the pony trail in the truck. "Let's go see what home looks like."

Dave had told me the job came with a house. He'd described a half-decent place, a former mine assayer's office, painted brown and yellow and here it was: A big pine curled up and over a gable roof. Behind the house, the cone of a mine dump climbed steadily toward the ridge top. Beyond the cabin, a weathered outhouse leaned against itself.

I pulled the truck onto a wedge of level ground and shut off the engine. Wooly and Zoom whined eagerly. "Yeah, guys," I added. "Home. At least for the moment."

Fortified by my companions' doggie enthusiasm, I walked up the path to the front porch and peered in the window. The floors were bare pine tongue and groove, and the walls were covered with pasted-on layers of yellowed newsprint. A black cook stove formed the centerpiece of the kitchen. A straight column of stovepipe rose from the firebox and disappeared through the ceiling and a straight-back chair stood by the stove.

The pine by the front porch stirred amiably. I put my hand on the doorknob and turned. The door creaked open on horror-show hinges and I stepped inside. Light streamed through the window and covered the stove in warmth. Sunlit dust hung in the air.

A fly buzzed against the window.

A crow laughed in the distance.

Wooly and Zoom scoured the yard, muzzles to the ground, tails held high, inhaling a new universe of smells. Across the road, a creek carried the spring runoff past my door and down the canyon.

I pulled the chair out into the sunlight. *Maybe this is going to pay off,* I thought. No concrete, no refinery, no nightmare war. No cops to hate, no trouble with a girlfriend. Time could stop here. The world could get along without me. I wanted to get along without the world.

The crow laughed again. "Fool."

"Fine," I replied. "I'll play the fool for you." I sat staring at the abandoned mine across the road. I felt my limbs begin to loosen while the sun-soaked quiet gently brought me down from the trip.

HAZEL

I awoke to the crunch of tires on gravel. Wooly and Zoom dashed around the corner of the cabin, barking wildly. A fragile-looking woman backed out of the driver's seat of a faded Jeep Cherokee. She was bundled in a red windbreaker and wore sensible shoes beneath her blue polyester pants. A funky red stocking cap perched on her steel-gray hair.

I walked down to meet her. She appraised me through blue-gray eyes.

This must be Hazel, I thought. My boss. Yikes.

She cocked her head to one side like a curious bird. "You're not him."

"I'm not who?" I asked, confused.

"We were expecting another fella."

"Ohh. Right." I laughed uneasily. "You were expecting Dave West."

She nodded brightly. "Fine young man. Very good with his hands, and . . ." Hazel added with controlled emphasis, ". . .from a fine Denver family."

A fine Denver family. The Dave West I knew had long, dirty-blond hair tied down with a bandanna. He smoked pot like a fiend and — when he wasn't doing finish carpentry work for rich folks — he sat at his kitchen table drinking coffee and strumming tunes on a Gibson guitar. After noon he switched to beer and sang out of tune, butchering his own scabbed-together lyrics. When Dave didn't have a guitar in hand he rubbed his wife, Toni, from neck to ankle while she purred obligingly. Dave West didn't have strong opinions about war, resistance, or society in general.

He was part of the parade of white, middle-class guys who had followed the '60s drumbeat — part of the way, part of the time. They might take a baby step or two toward resistance, but they all wore parachutes. He would cut his hair and suffer the loss the way a surfer mourns the end of summer. Then he would pull the ripcord and float down into the American Dream, morphing his rebellious forays into wistful nostalgia.

Like me, Dave had learned carpentry from his old man, but there, the similarity stopped. Dave's dad taught him how to win friends and influence people, how to succeed in business without trying, how to go after what he wanted without questioning his motives or direction. My old man had spent most of my adolescence looking for work. A bright but crazy electrical genius, he had had turned down a scholarship at M.I.T. to go to work as a radio operator on a succession of fishing boats, freighters, and passenger liners. During the Great Depression, he joined the Communist party, as had so many of the best and brightest in those dark days.

By the time the war ended and the McCarthy Era began, my old man couldn't get a security clearance. Blacklisted and without a degree, he was forced to seek a niche as a helter-skelter electrical engineer, a vacuum-tube ubermeister cum machinist, a Gyro Gearloose inventor. He was much admired but was always the first to go when his medical colleagues couldn't keep him attached to a government-funded research project. Stressed out by perpetual job-loss jeopardy, he would return from work to lie on the couch, arm thrown across his face. My father, this bright, debilitated man, had died at his own hand.

Hazel's extended hand brought me out of my reverie. "And you are . . ."

"Gus." I took her cool, papery hand in mine. "Gus Bessemer at your service. I take it you're Mrs. Gunther."

"Miss," she replied and took my hand. "I never did marry. Just didn't seem to have the time for it. And you can call me Hazel."

You could cut the gentility with a knife.

Smiling thinly, Hazel pushed past me and disappeared into the cabin. She walked straight through the little space and pushed open the back door.

I followed.

"Oh, dear," she exclaimed.

The sagging, water-stained walls of a dilapidated back shed tilted inwards. The roof was missing. The steep pitch of the mine dump careened toward us from the ridge top above.

"And so, Mister Bessemer. How would you proceed?" Hazel's head wobbled slightly.

"With what?"

"With rebuilding this back shed." Only a fool or an optimist would consider any alternative to tearing down the ruined shed. But I assumed this was a test, so I stepped into the debris. "First, I'd haul away all this wreckage. Next, I'd build a retaining wall to keep back that loose soil. And a foundation using this rock."

"They don't call them the Rockies for nothing, do they?" Hazel turned those gray-blue eyes on me. "The best stonemasons were the Welshmen," she continued. "Welshmen did the stonework in all the mines. You look to the Odd Fellows' Hall, Mister Bessemer. I think you'll be impressed. The power of more than seventy snows hasn't moved that building one inch. My father always said to look to the Welshmen. It was in their bones, he used to say."

"Yes, ma'am, I replied.

"I don't suppose you're a Welshman, are you, Mister Bessemer?"

"No ma'am. I grew up in New England. We have plenty of stones back there, too."

"New England." She looked at me sideways, perhaps to catch a clearer view of who I was. "I attended Bryn Mawr. Not exactly New England, but I hope to pass muster in your Yankee estimation."

Her eyes twinkled but I knew that I was the person who had to pass muster.

"Come with me." I extended my hand. She took it. A hopeful gesture. I ushered her out the front door and down the driveway. I pointed to the well-crafted redwood camper perched on the back of my pickup. "I built that," I said. "I can build anything you need. I can fix your plumbing. Need a roof fixed, I can do it. I can pour cement and build a fence. I take pride in my work. Look at this . . ."

I opened the side compartments on the Chevy and there, stacked neatly in the truck's metal bins, were my plumbing and mechanics tools. I showed her my finish-carpenter's bench with its planes, saws, framing square, and drill bits neatly tucked away in custom-fit cubicles. A tape, my 16- and 20-ounce hammers, and a brace of nail sets peeked out of the leather pockets of my tool belt and sunlight gleamed off the mahogany and brass of my spirit level. I grinned like an ape. "I can build anything you need," I repeated.

"I like the red star, Mister Bessemer. Quite festive. And the painted handprint is reminiscent of the habit the plains Indians had of claiming victory." She turned to me. "Do you claim victory, Mister Bessemer?"

Well, ma'am, I . . ."

Hazel watched the crow swoop into the pine that arched over the cabin. Its weight bent the treetop. "Big fellow," she said and turned back to me. "Are you married, Gus?"

"No, I . . ."

"Then you know how to cook." Hazel dove into the front seat of her Cherokee.

I stood in my tracks, too stunned to move. Had I passed the Dave West test?

She returned carrying a wicker basket and a package wrapped in blood-stained butcher paper. "Venison," she explained. "Mister Tallman brings me a nice supply for the winter. I'm a vegetarian of course and Mister Tallman doesn't know that, but I do so appreciate the gesture." She opened a basket full of fresh-baked rolls. "You'll need to warm your hearth," she advised.

I tore into the warm rolls while Hazel chatted on. My first assignment would be to look over her "commercial property," one of the broken-down storefronts opposite the Odd Fellows' Hall. "A few minor repairs should bring it up to snuff," she assured me as I walked her back to her Cherokee. "We'll see how you progress. I wondered who "we" was. I didn't see anybody else around. But all on her own, she let me know I wasn't hired yet — not by a long shot.

"Fuck it," I said to the dogs after Hazel left. Relinquishing my stranglehold on speculation, I unloaded the mattress from the truck, my sleeping bag, and the few pots and pans, dishes and cups I had stolen from Katie's California kitchen. I stacked my books and guitar next to the mattress.

After I completed setting up my Spartan household, I took out my Chinese coins and threw the *I Ching*. I had never been able to figure out why I put any stock in this pack of soothsayer vagaries. A stern, feudal, and patriarchal tome, it had been assembled by philosopher despots who had imposed serfdom, starvation, bound feet, and sanctioned prenuptial rape on endless generations of poor Chinese peasants.

So, what was I doing, sitting cross-legged in the sunlight, throwing coins onto the splintered pine floor of a mountain cabin? Throwing the *I Ching* coins supposedly sampled a moment in time. Millennia of thought had gone into deciphering the moment in the tumbled patterns of coins, yarrow stalks, or the cracks in a fire-ravaged tortoise shell. The *I Ching* was energized by the power of synchronicity and drew upon the symbolism of the collective unconscious, a laugh in the face of scientific process. Jung wrote about the *I Ching*. He believed it turned Western rational notions of cause and effect upside down and he applauded its structure and content.

For me, the truth was simpler. My personal life was a mess. No matter how clearly I could interpret the material world, anything that would cut through the mist that pervaded my heart and soul was worth a throw of the dice, or — in this case — the coins.

I threw *Yu*, or enthusiasm. Here, the arousing thunder resounds over the receptive earth. Cool. The ancient kings made music, offered it to the supreme deity — whatever that was — and invited their ancestors to party. "A prolonged state of tension is resolved," the well-worn pages told me. No shit, Shakespeare.

The sun fell behind the ridge top, taking the temperature with it. I needed to get that stove cooking or I would freeze. Springtime in the Rockies. Across the road, a stack of logs leaned against an abandoned mine shed. I pulled a couple of eight-footers off the stack and humped them to the cabin in the gathering darkness, hoping not to be discovered. I pulled out my only saw, a fine-tooth carpenter's tool and hacked away at the first log.

"You gotta be kidding me!"

I spun around to face a skinny character with a thick beard, hair laced into a pony tail. I had seen him earlier, gliding downhill in the blue pickup. The beard framed his thin-lipped mouth and acne scars stitched his olive skin.

"What're ya doin' there, brother?" He pointed at the pine log I had stolen from the abandoned mine across the road.

"I needed firewood."

"I can see that. What I wanna know is . . .Why're you buckin' firewood with that bread knife?" He broke into laughter.

"I'm a carpenter. It's what I got." My heartbeat settled down. "You always sneak up on people?"

"That's the way they do it out here." He stuck out a hand covered with scabs, calluses, and pine pitch. "Name's Malfese. John Malfese. I live right up the street. Only here, we call it 'a road.' I live 'up the road a piece.' " He roared with delight. "Quaint, ain't it?"

Malfese's truck was piled high with silver-gray pine logs. "Where'd you get all that wood?"

"Uh-uh. No way." He wagged his finger. "Trade secret." He howled like a dog.

Wooly and Zoom howled back.

"You may not know where I got my wood but . . ." He nodded at the log I had wedged onto the sawhorse. "I know where you got that shit."

I shrugged. "I just got here."

"Hey, man, forget about it." Malfese retied his ponytail. "Nobody's used that mine for years. Johnny won't do anything about it 'cept preach.

"Who's Johnny?"

"Johnny LaPorte. Coolest town marshal this side of Gunsmoke."

"So he's not gonna bust me for this?"

"He'll notice all right, but he's not gonna bother. Marshal Johnny LaPorte, he's got bigger fish to fry."

"Cool," I said, relaxing my defensive position. "I'm working for this old lady, you probably know her, Hazel? Hazel Gunther?"

"Hazel, huh?" He laughed. "The old broad owns half the town." Malfese scratched his beard. "She's good people, Hazel. A little bit nuts, but so's everybody else up here. You got to be. It's a survival thing."

"What do you mean?"

"Look at me. I'm a city boy. Last year, hot time, summer in the city, I get into a jam of a business nature. No way out. So, I jump in my Caddy and riiiiiide." He did a little dance in the twilight.

"Cadillac?" I looked past him at the beat up old International.

"Yeah, brother, Ca-di-llac. I was livin' good. Wine, women, song, et cet-e-ra." He emphasized each syllable. "However, my former colleagues, not being so much into peace and love as am I, they begin to adopt a life-and-death type of a attitude towards me. So, I say to my self, time to get outta the Bronx. I start drivin' and I'm so damn high, I keep going until the Cadillac gets jammed in a snow drift right down the road. A bunch of hippies pull me out and presto! Smart-ass dope dealer becomes smart-ass mountain man! A month later I sell the Caddie and bought that International. But enough o' that shit."

Malfese disappeared around the corner of the cabin. I heard the rip snort of a two-stroke motor jump into action and the mountain man walked back into the lantern light brandishing a chainsaw like an M-1 carbine. If he'd been smoking a cigar, this jovial ex-dope dealer could have stepped out of the Sierra Maestra with Che and Fidel.

"You don't have to do this."

He drowned me out with the chain saw. "Camaahn!" he shouted over the racket. "Whaddya think neighbors are for? Beside, I can't stand to watch a guy make a fool of himself." He pushed me out of the way and dropped the chainsaw blade onto the log I had nested in the rickety sawhorse. Wood chips flew. "Cuttin' firewood with a handsaw. Shit."

In less than a minute he had reduced my liberated logs into a pile of firebox-length pine stubs. "You got a axe?"

I nodded.

"That stuff'll split like smokestack lightnin', man."

"Thanks for the help," I said. "I woulda been out here all night."

"Don't mention it." Malfese threw the chain saw in the back of the truck. "We all pull together around here. Got to. You'll see."

It was dark by the time I split the wood and fired up the stove. I lit candles. As the cabin began to warm, I found a frazzled broom in the wreckage of the back shed and swept the cabin floor. I seared Hazel's venison in my skillet and poured canned beans and molasses into my other pan. I hauled water up from the creek and set it on the stove for coffee. I was feeling like a regular Davy Crockett when the door rattled under the flat of a hand.

I flung the door open.

A guy as big as a barn blocked the scenery. He was dressed in overalls and a blue-and-white chambray shirt the thickness of sailcloth. A white flat-top Stetson clamped his forehead, tugged and twisted into shape by constant tugging at the brim. He looked like a giant caught halfway between adolescence and adulthood.

The giant held a lit, glass-bottomed kerosene lantern in each hand. The light cast eerie shadows on his broad, pudgy features. "Didn't mean to disturb your meal. Seen your candle in the window," he said. "Looked pathetic. Decided I better get down here and shed a little light on the subject. Hee hee." He said "hee hee" in two distinct words.

I let him in.

"Left the place pretty clean, didn't they?" He peered around the interior of the cabin.

"You know the people who lived here before?" I was curious. I had gotten a strong hit off the place, a shadow of leathery miners, Victorian, closed-off, crazy but nothing recent.

"Folks lived here up till couple of months ago. Patrick and his old lady — Mary her name was." He spoke of her as if she was dead. "And a coupla kids. Showed up last summer in a potato chip van. They didn't last the winter."

"Here." I pulled the chair near the stove. "Siddown." I was beginning to feel claustrophobic next to the towering mass of this guy.

"So this guy, Patrick . . ." The giant straddled the chair, dwarfing it. "His wife took it 'til one Saturday last March." He set the lamps on the edge of the stove and lit them. "It's always the women got the sense to throw in the towel. They make it through the winter, but soon as the weather breaks, somethin' snaps." He took out a cigar and lit it off the heat rising from the lamp chimney. "After the women leave, the fella hangs around for a week or two. Then they realize what it's like to live alone up here and they're gone, like thieves in the night. Weeds out the wise ones from the fools." He pulled on his cigar for emphasis. "The wise ones move on. The fools stick around. Hee hee." He giggled again and looked at me. "Which will you be, I wonder?"

I handed him the bottle of brandy and looked down at the lanterns. They cast a clean, white yellow light in the room. "I'm grateful for the lamps. How much do I owe you?"

"You owe me two lamps. When you get around to it. Cut the lamp wicks at a forty-five degree angle like you see 'em here. That way, they don't smoke up and you don't have to wash 'em. You don't have to wash 'em, you won't break 'em. Least, that's the way it goes with me. But then, there I go. Name's Norman. Norman Bowkers."

When I told him I had come from the Bay Area, Norman raised his eyebrows. "You a hippie, a revolutionary, or a draft dodger?"

I assessed the big man sitting on my only chair. Norman had hands big enough to punch me right through the door and it was cold outside. "Maybe I'm all three," I said.

"Whatever. No never mind to me. You may think you're livin' in the middle of nowhere, but a lot of folks come and go. All kinds. Everybody body's got a story, but we tend to play our cards close to the chest up here. And we tend to play fair." Norman Bowkers stood up, casting a shadow against the wall and ceiling. "Be seein' ya."

REALITY

The next day, I threw my fate to the dogs and drove down Left Hand Canyon Road to Boulder. The road dropped precipitously for a few miles, then evened into a gentle descent through the sun-warmed pines of the foothills. As I neared Boulder, tidy summer homes took over for the rough-and-tumble architecture of Montgomery's shanties.

The eastern slope of the Rockies lurches out of the high plains in a row of granite slabs called the Flatirons. From Denver westward, the Flatirons angle into the blue sky in frozen tribute to the convulsion that pushed the Rocky Mountains out of the earth's crust. Boulder was half farm town, half college town, snuggled up against these great, sky bound stones. Ranchers, farmers, and mechanics cruised Main Street in pickups. Cowboys, bargirls, and students crowded the sidewalks.

I found a supermarket and bought $20 worth of beans, bread, beer, cheese, rice, and looked for the nearest hardware store. I found one on Main Street, complete with wood floors worn smooth by boots, handcarts, and merchandise. Nails came in a barrel and you bought them by the pound. The kerosene sat in a fifty-five gallon drum turned sideways on an iron sawhorse. The clerk behind the counter looked at me from between big ears.

"Hi," I said.

"Howdy," he said.

"I need kerosene."

Silence.

"Do you sell it by the gallon or do you sell it in a can, or what?"

The clerk stared at me, jaws working a wad of chewing tobacco. He picked up a coffee can, spat, and wiped his mouth on his shirtsleeve. "What was that again?"

I looked around. A rancher and a clerk guffawed as they measured lengths of chain with a yardstick. Were they laughing at me? "Kerosene." I was the only guy in the joint with long hair. I wanted to get out of there.

"Right over there." He nodded toward the barrel.

"I need something to put it in."

The clerk disappeared behind a faded green curtain.

The men at the chain spool guffawed again. My hair rippled in the breeze from a fan set behind the counter.

The clerk returned with a two-gallon can. "Got a spigot you can pull out for the pourin'. Nothin' worse than gettin' kerosene on the kitchen table. Missus'll give ya hell. Course you don't look like you got a missus."

"Yeah, yeah, I know." I said. "I look like I am the missus."

"You said it, I didn't," he said. "Dollar thirty-four with tax."

The early evening lights of Boulder spread out over the plains. Everyone seemed to have a place to go, a body to be with. I regretted the choice I had made; a week ago, I belonged someplace, with somebody. I called Katie collect.

She refused the call. I dropped a quarter in the slot and dialed again.

She picked up. I could hear the kids playing in the background.

"They came after you," Katie said.

"What?" I asked. "Who?"

"The FBI guys. And the local cops. They scared the kids half to death."

"You didn't have to let them in, ya know."

"They pushed right past me. Said they didn't need a warrant . . ."

"Bullshit."

"Three plainclothesmen, two Richmond cops, and the landlord. You tell them 'bullshit' if you want. Me, I let them in. They searched the whole house with gloves on, like we were infected."

Long distance hissed between us through the wires. I could see Katie leaning against the wall by the phone. "Are the kids okay?"

"Yeah, they're all right. I told them you hadn't done anything wrong and that we just want to change the world."

"Did they get it?"

"They already know it. They believe in it."

The operator cut in so I fed a couple more quarters into the slot.

"The kids think we're good people," Katie said.

"Don't you think we're good people?"

"Oh shut up, Gus. I'm a mom. I had cops laying attitude on me like I was a left-wing tramp." Pause. "They found your clothes. They know you live here."

"Look, Katie. This thing will blow over. They just want to hassle the people they tagged at People's Park."

"I don't want to hear about it," Katie said. "You hear that, guys?" She directed the question to unseen wire tappers. "I don't know what he did and I don't know where he is. Hear that fellas? It's all over now."

"Katie, I . . ."

The operator cut in. "Please deposit . . .

"Take care of yourself, Gus."

I listened to the dial tone for a moment and hung up.

I drove up the darkened canyon, desolation trading places with anger. I couldn't help but soak up Katie's humiliation. The Man had forced his way into the sanctity of her home — our home — and had run his fingers through her dirty laundry. I was a criminal. Katie was a whore. We lived on no money with grace and simplicity, they drew federal paychecks and wore gloves in my house. They were cleaning out a nest of filthy — dangerous — insects. We were the insects.

I was used to it. I had grown up Commie in the McCarthy Era. I knew how dangerous belief could be. As a child, I heard the pounding on my door, hollering incoherently about commies and bastards. I heard the muffled conversations between my parents as the FBI came and went. I watched television heroes like Sergeant Friday on "Dragnet" wipe out nests of communists as if they were vermin. I struggled to reconcile my parents' politics with the characters who were clearly the bad guys on television, but who also looked like my parents and their friends.

I felt bad for Katie. Beneath her anger and defiance, she was a nice, middle-class girl. She had roots in the world of Chryslers and Kelvinators. As a child, she had sat in front of the television on Sunday nights and wished upon a star. Her dad was a teacher, her mother a housewife. The system worked for them, feeding them, protecting them, shaping their dreams as they nestled in the shadow of a malevolent giant. Even if you've felt the shadow of authority before, it's hard not to feel like a piece of shit when the Man comes busting into your home.

QUILLS AND PLIERS

Wooly and Zoom lay on the porch, waiting for me. I lit a lamp and my heart fell. Quills again. In the lamp-lit sphere, my dogs looked like the Saint Sebastian twins, canine martyrs shot through with tormentors' arrows. They waited, forlorn, resigned to their pain.

I fought back panic. What would I do this time? Turn around and drive back down the canyon? It was too late to find a vet, two hours away in Boulder. I loaded my pain-filled recidivists into the back of the truck. Both dogs whined but they were too weak and weary to object. "We'll get you out of this," I promised and ground up the hill in second gear, looking for signs of life.

Ed's Peak to Peak café boasted electricity, indoor plumbing and a paved parking lot. It stood at the top of the hill overlooking the town. In contrast to the ramshackle anarchy of the cabins below it, the café looked tight and prosperous. Light splashed out of the windows onto a broad front porch. Timbers and trim gleamed with spar varnish and forest-green enamel. A collection of busted-out pickup trucks, station wagons, and one yellow VW bug with a blackened fender cozied up to a hitching rail that ran the length of the building. I shut off the engine.

Raucous laughter rattled the windowpanes.

I gave the pups a pat and climbed the stairs to meet the townspeople of Montgomery.

I opened the door and stepped into the light. The laughter and hubbub subsided. Faces turned towards me like a chorus of full moons. Men and women dressed in jeans, wool shirts, down vests, and a diverse array of hats lounged in the café's knotty pine booths. A potbellied stove stood in the middle of the room.

A tall, lantern-jawed man with sandy hair and steel-rimmed glasses stood behind a lunch counter. He raised his hand in silent greeting.

"That's Ed." Norman stood up from one of the booths. "He owns the place." He turned to the assembly. "And this . . ." He slapped my shoulder. "This is the guy I told you about."

Wow. What had he told them?

Norman turned to me. "Never did get your name," he said.

"Gus," I said. "My name's Gus." I held off on the last name. "Just got here."

"And he already got himself a house and a job," Malfese said. "Not bad, brother."

I shrugged noncommittally. I hadn't got the nod from Hazel and I didn't know how the locals would take my sudden appearance.

"You met Malfese," Norman said. He nodded toward the woodcutter.

Thanks for the hand," I said to Malfese.

"Glad to meet you all." I jumped in fast. For all I knew, somebody here in the café could lay claim to the mine timbers I had hoisted. "I'm down the canyon, in one of Hazel's. . ."

"We know," said a burly, round-faced guy shaved painfully pink and topped off by a navy-surplus seaman's watch cap. He put out his hand. "Name's Buster." He sat in a booth next to a pretty, olive-skinned woman with thick, dark hair."

"I'm Cheryl." She smiled. "I live here, too."

My dogs were in the truck, hurting, and I needed help. Soon. "Dave was going to take the job himself," I explained, "but something came up."

"Lotta people know how to swing a hammer up here," said a tall, black-haired guy with a thick beard. Even in his mountain gear, he looked like an aristocrat. "Maybe we need a union."

"That's Reisinger," Norman said. "Some day, if he gets over all this foolishness," he continued, "he's gonna make one helluva lawyer."

"You may not have a problem," I said. "Hazel made it pretty clear I'm on probation."

"You need the job?" Buster asked.

"I had gas money to get here." The image of my stricken dogs pushed me forward. "Me and my dogs . . ."

"Shit. Just what this fuckin' town needs." A skinny kid with scruffy hair and a rusty beard turned on his stool at the counter. "An outta town carpenter with a buncha dogs."

"Look," I said. "Sorry if I took a job away from you. Nobody told me anything about your town. Sounded like a good place to get away for a while."

Malfese, the woodcutter I'd met earlier, guffawed. "Lotsa luck."

"How's that?" asked Buster.

"Just needed time to think things over," I said. "Back in San Francisco . . ."

"Fuckin' flatlander." The skinny, scruffy kid sucked on his Budweiser.

"Take a pill, Sullivan," Cheryl said. "Hazel wouldn't hire you no matter what."

"Peace, my children," said Malfese. "The universe is, no doubt, unfolding it as it should."

I could feel my dogs hurting in the truck. "Sorry to bust in on your party, but I need some advice," I said. "My dogs got into porcupines."

"Uh-oh," said Cheryl.

"It's like pussy," said Sullivan. "Once they get the taste . . ."

"Oh for chrissakes, Sullivan." A pretty, round-faced woman with an overbite leaned back behind the counter. "What do you know about pussy?"

People laughed and I felt my shoulders settle a little.

"Hi," the pretty, round-faced woman said. "And welcome to Montgomery. They call me Jewel and you don't have to pay any attention to the bad vibes." She turned to the assembly. "These guys are just hosing down the hydrant."

Jewel looked as if she had been drawn by a cartoonist who loved women — dark, earnest eyes, a smattering of freckles across her cheeks, smooth skin over a rounded body. She'd tugged her hair back into a thick pair of braids.

"Bring in your dogs," Cheryl said.

"Yeah," Buster added. "We'll have a quill-pulling party." He turned to the café owner. "That okay with you, Ed?"

"Sure." Ed pulled a stack of newspapers off the counter and tossed them on the red-and-black squares of the linoleum floor. "Just keep your hounds on the papers."

Jewel and pink-faced Buster followed me out to the truck. I lifted Zoom up and over the tailgate.

Buster scooped Zoom into his gargantuan arm span with surprising tenderness.

"'At's okay, baby," Jewel crooned. "We're gonna fix ya up." She reached out to stroke Zoom's forlorn eyebrows exposing a splint and a bandage on her middle finger.

"What happened to you?" I asked.

"Shaved my knuckle. Cuttin' kindling. It's dangerous up here." She looked straight into my eyes. "Course, not so dangerous as where you been."

"Where's that?" I asked.

"Over there," she said. "The war."

I frowned. Jesus H. Christ! What was I putting out? The veterinarian, now this Jewel chick. I hadn't been overseas. Quite the contrary. I followed Jewel and Buster back up the café stairs, grateful for the aid and comfort.

Inside, the crowd made the dogs nervous. They stood strong, heads down, front paws braced, growling.

"Those dogs are a mess," said a reedy voice from a corner booth. "Why don't you put 'em out of their misery?"

I looked to see if the speaker was joking. Nobody had introduced him. His milky gray eyes shifted wolf-like and strands of beard ran down his cheeks like dirty water. "Hey, Brucie," Jewel snapped. "We could put you out of your misery, too."

Sullivan returned from his truck with a pair of pliers. Ed produced a row of Budweisers to fortify the surgeons. Buster brought in a bottle of whiskey. He handed the bottle to Norman, who took a swig, grabbed Wooly between his knees, and poured a slug of the brown fluid down the dog's throat. Wooly gagged and recoiled.

"That'll knock the poor bastard out," Norman explained. "Otherwise he'll fight like a banshee. Besides . . ." Norman took another hit of the whiskey, grabbed the pliers and approached Zoom. "I'm gonna need it myself."

The dogs growled and twisted; they whined and bucked but we held them like miniature broncos while Norman steered the pliers onto each barb and tugged. Blood and quills built up on the newspapers in a mess of gore. A half hour later, two exhausted dogs lay panting under the booths. They'd been picked clean of quills. Almost.

"Those broken ones, they'll be workin' themselves out for the next coupla weeks," Norman explained. "But they'll survive."

Drained by the bloody ordeal, people began to leave. I helped Jewel and Ed clean up the kitchen while I let the dogs rest. "So the way people were talking . . . I can look forward to this happening again?" I asked.

"I don't know," said Ed. "I'm from Chicago. That was a first for me."

"Jeez," I replied. "They look like pulling quills was something they did every day."

"Everything they do up here looks like they do it every day," said Jewel.

"People around here," Ed said. "They know how to work together. It just happens. They may seem rough-edged at first, but they're pretty well worn in with each other." He bid us goodnight and reminded Jewel to lock up on the way out.

"You work here?" I asked.

"Everybody works for Ed, one time or another." She walked behind the counter and doused the coffee machine. "So what's the red star all about?"

"Huh?"

"On your truck. You got a red star on your door. What's it about?"

"Not much," I said.

"Okay," Jewel conceded. "And what about the hands?"

"The Sioux used to cover their palms with dye and daub it on the flanks of their ponies," I said.

"You an Indian?" she asked.

"No," I answered.

"So what do you need hands on your horse for?"

"It's just a sign, that's all." I considered the Lakota Sioux to be part of the great American guerrilla movement. What did Jewel think? It was too early to know which way the wind blew in the mountains of Colorado. They could all have rifles and American flags in their pickups for all I knew. For the time being, I'd keep my politics to myself.

She regarded me with light amusement. "Shit, man. Forget I asked. Keep your secret. I was just curious." She headed for the door. "Let's get your dogs in the truck and you can take me down to my place."

I scooped Zoom up in my arms and Wooly wobbled along behind us, tail drooping. We drove down the hill in silence.

"Here. Stop here. This is me."

I pulled over. Jewel had been the woman in the long skirt who had waved to me when I first drove into town, one short day ago. A bell clanked softly in the darkness.

"My goat," she explained.

"Thanks for your help," I said. "And I appreciate your curiosity."

"You may not know it yet, but you're among friends," she said. "If you want 'em."

"Just so this thing doesn't snowball," I said. "I'm not a vet. I haven't been to Vietnam. As a matter of fact, I worked pretty hard to stay away from Vietnam."

"You won't find me giving you any shit about it."

"It's not like I blame anybody."

"Better not. Bad karma."

"Fucking draft. Most of those poor bastards over there, they get dragged into this thing. Weird thing is, most of them don't kick or scream. If they say anything it's in defense of God and country and fighting commies . . . crap like that. Sure isn't about their own arms and legs." I stared at my hands on the steering wheel. "They go quiet. Quiet and pissed off."

"How do you know?"

"I stood outside the Oakland Induction Center plenty of times when the busses would pull up. 'You don't have to go,' we'd say. Guys in their crew cuts and madras shirts. Guys from the ghetto. They would shoulder you, try to sucker punch you, call you a commie or a traitor. But most of them, they just shuffle into that induction center and Presto! they're gone. But if you catch them, they all have this look…"

"What look?"

Scared, hateful, wild-eyed. Like cattle getting shoved down a chute."

"How come you didn't have to go?"

"I got a chance to see it from a different angle."

"Meaning . . ."

"I talked my way out. Went up against my draft board. But that's another story." I didn't want to spill the whole pot of beans. "Anyhow, whatever you think, I'm no vet."

Up the slope past Jewel's cozy cabin, a white-clapboarded church or town hall glowed in the moonlight.

"Didn't somebody come up with something like… 'girls say 'yes' to guys who say 'no'?" Jewel grinned.

"Yeah. It's a slogan. On an antiwar poster. It's a picture of Joan Baez and her sister and another chick."

"I liked it."

Was Jewel propositioning me? Tilly called me from over the mountains. I started my truck.

"Hey, it's just a saying," Jewel said. "Take it any way you want to." She put her hand on the door. "It doesn't matter. The whole war thing sucks."

"You're right." The night sky swirled with stars, the same stars that looked down on the other side of the planet, torn by fire and sword, shrapnel and napalm, so far away. "The whole war thing does suck," I repeated. "I just wanted to set the record straight, that's all. About the Vietnam vet thing and all."

"And all." Her eyes glistened in the solo light of Montgomery's only street light. "You're a funny guy, Gus," she said. "Take your dogs and go lie down." She got out of the truck and caught me admiring the curve of her ass. She gave a short, bright laugh. "I got to feed my goat," she said and slammed the truck door.

HAZEL'S STOREFRONT

With its false front and rusted tin roof, Hazel's commercial property looked straight out of a Western on a Hollywood back lot. It was a mess. Half a century of spring melt-off had eaten through the foundation. Sagging stairs clung to the doorjamb, winter storms had burnished the fir siding to a silver-toned velvet. I ducked into the basement, took a quick look at the clutter of timbers wedging up the sagging floor joists and ducked back out into the sunlight. Terminally ill, I thought. I didn't want to cheat the old lady out of a summer's wages by propping up a dead horse.

I found Hazel in her back yard, wrangling mops in a bucket.

"Mister Bessemer." Hazel set down the bucket and cradled the mop handles in her elbow. "How goes the battle?" There was a gleam in her eye.

"Miz Gunther, I've been poking around underneath that building of yours."

"Nothing a little elbow grease can't take care of, eh?"

"Well, actually, uh . . ." Here goes. I "I don't think elbow grease is going to get the job done."

"In your estimation."

I got a fleeting impression — not of a wary property owner — but of a randy schoolgirl. Hazel was a flirt. She was checking me out. A good sign. "Yes, ma'am. In my estimation."

"Oh, dear," Hazel said. "Would you like some lemonade?" Before I could reply, Hazel disappeared into her pantry. "Just make yourself comfortable on the verandah," she called.

I picked my way through an obstacle course of doily-covered armchairs. The dining room table was piled high with papers, magazines, and correspondence. The "verandah" was a glassed-in front porch that surveyed the canyon below. I sat down in a swinging sofa that creaked like a bed frame.

Across the road, a fireplug of a man in blue jeans and a red-and-black checked shirt clambered into a red '48 Ford pickup.

"That's Eddie Warren," Hazel said from behind a pitcher of iced tea. "His folks built that cabin. Eddie, even though he's just a boy like you."

I liked that. 'Just a boy.' Maybe she'd cut me some slack.

"Eddie likes to keep the old ways. Quite the hard-rock miner too, I'm told."

She handed me a tumbler of lemonade. "Squeeze it myself from fresh lemons and keep it in the root cellar. Temperature's always just right down there."

The sun had warmed up the day and I was beginning to sweat in my heavy shirt. The lemonade went down cool.

"So . . ." She seated herself on the swing beside me. "Tell me of your concerns."

"I don't have much hope for the place, Miz Gunther. The foundations are gone."

"That would be the snow," Hazel explained. "These winters . . ."

"I'm sure they're fierce."

"Fierce. Yes. That's the word for it. Fierce. Of course there's more to it than snow." She winked at me confidentially. "There's the wind, you see."

"Well, that brings me to my point, Miz Gunther."

"You should call me Hazel. They all do. We don't stand on ceremony around here." She laughed. "We're all too busy to be calling each other 'mister this' or 'miss that,'" she said.

"Okay, Hazel. But the fact is, to repair that building, you'd be throwing good money after bad."

"I haven't thrown any money anywhere, Mister Bessemer." She took a sip of lemonade.

So there I was, sitting on a verandah two miles in the air, chatting with a little old lady who held a glass of lemonade in one hand and my welfare in the other.

"Why don't you rebuild it?"

"Come again?" I asked.

"The building. My commercial property. Tear it down and salvage the lumber. That's the way we did it in the Great Depression. Didn't waste a thing." Hazel smiled at me, bright-eyed, head wobbling on ancient tendons. "I do own the property y'know. That's where it all begins. With the land."

"Yes, ma'am," I said.

"My father used to say, 'Land. Buy land. Only thing in the world there isn't any more of.' Times change, but the land remains. Steady as a rock." She winked and took another sip of lemonade.

Wow. What a coquette. She was a cutie, even at eighty three.

"You'd have to demolish her carefully so you don't destroy the wood."

I couldn't believe my ears, but I seized the moment. "A lot of the wood seems good."

"You could store the salvaged lumber right across the road — in the Odd Fellows' Hall. And if you need help . . ."

Oh no, I thought. *You'll pitch in?*

"We could hire on the better sort of young people in the town." Hazel said. "You will need a new foundation."

Hazel took another sip of lemonade. "And I will want an estimate of your expenses."

"Of course." This was working out just fine.

"Yes," Hazel mused. "Our own little public works project. You know, Mister Roosevelt had ideas like these. My father didn't agree with Mister Roosevelt back then, but things change. Franklin Delano Roosevelt created all sorts of public works projects you know. Saved this country from succumbing to the dark forces of revolution. Quite a time, back then. Quite a man, that President Roosevelt."

When I brought my figures back to Hazel, she studied them for an eternity or two and nodded her head. That was it. I took her parchment-skinned hand in mine. On the strength of a handshake, this old woman was going to hire me to tear down her "commercial property" and rebuild it from the ground up.

I'd be lucky if I finished before the first snow fell.

The next morning I clambered up a ladder and crabbed my way along the corrugated spine of Hazel's tin roof. I leaned over the false front of the building and surveyed Montgomery spread away below me.

The sun had risen high above the ridge tops and the sky rang postcard blue. The air smelled clean. My skin, lungs, and muscles felt tight, clear, and big. My troubles lay a thousand miles behind. I was full of pancakes and coffee and I was going to construct a building from scratch and get paid for it.

I love tearing things apart. Poke a crowbar between wood and metal, jab between trim strip and roofing, search for a foothold for the leverage your body needs to rip a twelve-foot plank out of its resting place. Flex the muscles, wrench upward, wood fibers groaning, a rusty shriek. In that moment, nails that haven't seen the light of day for a hundred years emerge into sunlight. Rotten planks disintegrate in a shower of wood pulp and dust that blows away in the wind, matter transformed, flying free for the first time since it was photosynthesized.

Halfway down the pitch of Hazel's roof, a curl of rusty roofing bit me like a snake. Blood oozed out of a ragged flap of skin. Sucking on the crotch of my hand, sweat smarting my eyes, I climbed down to wash the wound and to pull my gloves out of the truck.

I was holding my torn flesh under a faucet when Jewel stopped, leaned a tanned and chubby arm out the window of her pickup and grasped the mirror frame like a guy. "Taking a break already?"

"How do you know when I began?"

"I was watching you." Jewel looked at my hand. "Oof," she said. "That looks like it smarts. I got stuff back at the house. You want to . . .?"

"No thanks," I interrupted.

"Suit yourself. Jesus. I didn't invite you over for a glass of champagne." Jewel laughed and threw me a piteous look.

I sucked at my hand.

"I gotta go," she said. "Need anything in town?"

"I got a whole list. I'll take care of it all tomorrow," I said between sucks.

"Boy, you're the self-reliant type, aren't you?" Jewel ground her dusty pickup into first gear. "That a matter of principle or are you just scared of girls?"

"Maybe both."

"Oooo. Mister Mystery here." She grinned. "Funny thing about Montgomery . . ."

"What's that?"

"You can hide out here. A lotta people do. But you can't disappear. You'll see." Jewel took off down the hill, waving gaily.

My confusion was mighty. I could have gone to Jewel's cabin. She might have taken my wounded hand in hers, washed it, bandaged it, kissed it. I might have caressed her smooth-skinned arm and shoulder, worked my fingers underneath the tight line of her t-shirt. I imagined Jewel without her clothes, that warm, self-assured smile on her face, eyes closed, brown body on white sheets. I sighed out loud, my warm breath ushering the daydream from my soul and away into the thin mountain air.

INVASION

The next night, Reisinger, the lawyer-to-be, pulled up in front of my cabin. His flatbed truck was filled with Montgomery's males, all primed to celebrate Buster's last days, weeks, or months of bachelorhood. Buster and Cheryl hadn't named the date but that didn't seem to dampen the enthusiasm for a night on the town. The mood was infectious. Somewhere between the resentment at my arrival and the quill-pulling episode, Montgomery's males had given me a thumbs up. Despite my intention to remain hermetically sealed in my work and my cabin, I climbed on board Reisinger's truck and we motored off down the canyon.

The town of Silver Hill lay in the soft curves of the foothills. It had a gentler, more recently painted façade than Montgomery. It pretended to be a mining town, but it clearly catered to flatlanders. Even the mine dumps seemed civilized. The Silver Hill Inn was an authentic old Victorian structure with a carved balustrades and broad, sheltered porch. The Inn sat behind a line of cast-iron hitching posts shaped like horse heads.

"How quaint," Reisinger mumbled.

"Whiskey's the same here as anywhere." Norman shouldered open the door and led the way. The rest of us tumbled out of Reisinger's truck and rumbled onto the broad porch, laughing and cursing and jostling one another.

Inside, wagon wheel candelabras hung from the rafters and herds of deer and elk antlers jutted from the walls. A massive, zinc-topped bar dominated the room and four-foot logs roared in a fieldstone fireplace.

At a table in a far corner, a circle of cowboys sat around a round oak table. They looked like extras on the set of "High Noon." Slouching in their chairs and fingering long-neck bottles of Coors, these foothill range riders were clad uniformly in blue jeans, plaid shirts, and down vests. All wore hats pushed back on their heads and sported mustaches.

The men from Montgomery clumped into the saloon, long hair and mud clinging to Levi's, Can't Bust 'Ems, and Ben Johnson coveralls slick with mechanic's grease and coal dust. Nothing matched from torn boots and busted-out dungarees to the slack-sleeved long underwear and an odd assortment of hats. We galumphed across the room and — as protocol would have it — bellied up to the bar.

A cowboy raised a beer above his head. "Outta the west, hippies! This is God's country!"

"The hell it is." Norman grinned a crooked grin and waved. "This land belongs to you and me, brother."

The Silver Hill men turned their backs. The table rumbled with locker-room laughter, but these guys had been out of high school for a long time.

I perched at the bar's brass rail. I caught Juicy Brucie Berenger, the guy nobody knew, eyeballing the cowboy table.

Brucie's eyes caught mine. He dropped his gaze. I hadn't seen him on Reisinger's truck. How did he get here? And why? He wasn't friends with Norman or Buster. Jewel said he wasn't friends with anybody. "Know those people?" I asked.

"Nah," he said and adjusted his neck with a crack of vertebrae.

"Gentlemen." Norman raised his glass. "We got business."

Malfese put his arm around Buster's neck. "Tonight we honor this man. For his bravery, his courage in a clinch. For actually managin' to coexist with a woman."

"She keeps me warm at night." Buster's heart wasn't in the cliché. Machismo wasn't his strong suit.

"Cheers." Norman grinned and knocked back his beer. "This man's gettin' married in the mornin'. Some mornin' comin' up directly." The grin fell. "Uh-oh."

A pretty, short-haired, dark-eyed woman shot into the saloon and headed straight for the bar.

"Ann," Reisinger muttered.

"And without the kid," said Norman.

Flanked by Jewel and Cheryl, Reisinger's wife, Ann, shoved a couple of Montgomery men aside and ordered beers and whiskeys.

"Ann, honey." Reisinger said. "What are you doin' here?"

"Whatever I damned well please," she replied.

"This is supposed to be a stag party!" Sullivan complained.

"There's your stag party." Cheryl jerked a thumb toward the mass of antlers and dead animal heads nailed to the tavern walls. "Up against the wall, motherfuckers!"

The women shrieked with laughter.

Ann stalked to a table in the center of the room. "Theme for tonight, guys? Separate but equal."

Jewel hit me with a twitch of her hip. "Stick around," she said. "Coupla more drinks, we'll have made our point and you guys'll have bored yourselves to death."

"We already have," I said.

Jewel scooped up her drink and joined the other women at the table.

One of the cowboys pushed away from the table and strode over to the women. He leaned down and spoke to Ann.

Reisinger stiffened. "What's he think he's doin'?"

"Don't get all Neanderthal, Reisinger," Norman said. "Knowing those women, I'd let them handle it."

The women blinked up big-eyed at the cowboy.

Ann grabbed the cowboy's sleeve and whispered into his ear.

Cheryl added another line.

The cowboy straightened up — fast.

The women smiled sweetly.

The cowboy jammed his hands into his jeans pockets and took a long step away from the table.

"Look at him," Norman said. "He's blushing. Hee hee."

"Don't worry, cowboy." Ann stood up and spoke loud enough for all to hear. "You don't look near as stupid as you feel."

"You can tell your friends we were fighting over you." Cheryl nodded her head toward the cowboy's buddies.

Doused in laughter, the cowboy retreated to the bar. "Gimme a Jack Daniels, straight up."

Norman raised his eyebrows. "Only the best, huh, fella?"

"Somebody ought to teach them girls a lesson," he said.

"Oh, I wouldn't mess with them," Norman said.

"I hear they're from Montgomery," Reisinger added.

"Wouldn't doubt it," the dude said. "Bunch of dykes."

"Boy," Brucie said. "I wouldn't let those chicks push me around like that."

"Hey, dipshit . . . " The cowboy turned toward Brucie. "What's your problem?"

The table full of cowboys watched their buddy face off with Brucie.

"He don't have a problem, partner." Norman jerked Brucie away but his eyes stayed on the cowboy. "We're here to party, right, Brucie?"

The cowboy eyed the stag party. "Where you guys from?"

"Oh, here and there," Buster said.

"They're from Montgomery," Brucie said. "We all are."

"Assholes," the tall dude snarled through his mustache. "Bunch of fuckin' hippies."

"Wrong." Brucie wiped his nose with his sleeve. "If we was hippies we wouldn't be so eager to kick your Silver Hill ass."

I groaned.

Norman stepped between Brucie and the cowboy. He dwarfed them both. "Why don't you go back and join your friends, friend."

"Y'know, peace and love don't mean shit," Brucie continued. "Does it guys?"

Norman kicked Brucie hard, keeping his bulk in the tall dude's face.

"You sound pretty tough, standin' behind those two gorillas there." The cowboy sneered at Brucie. "Peace creeps." His eyes moved quickly, searching for allies. "Keep that shit up and you won't have a fuckin' town left. Montgomery, Colorado. Raggedy-assed little shithole's liable to blow away in the next good windstorm anyhow."

Cowboys from the corner table hit the bar, flanking Buster and Norman.

Somebody landed a fist on my cheekbone. I stumbled against the bar, then grabbed for the guy's wrists. He was a foot taller than me. He undercut my reach and punched me in the chest, knocking the wind out of me. I heard a glass shatter down the bar, the sound of fists on flesh, the scuffling of boots.

The bartender came around the counter with a baseball bat. He had a mustache as big as his belly and he was nervous. Not a good combination. "Come on, now fellas. We got folks eatin' dinner here."

"You people suck," Brucie shouted at the cowboys from the far end of the Montgomery phalanx.

Norman grabbed him by the shirt front. "Shut up, Brucie."

"Yoo hoo! Boys! You big, strong, handsome Montgomery men." Cheryl, Jewel, and Ann beckoned from their table. "Come on over here! We got something to show you!" Before we got our asses kicked again, we made our way to the table, leaving the Silver Hill cowboys to order a round from the nervous bartender.

"Good boys," Ann said, rubbing Reisinger's hairy forearm like he was a dog. "No fighting," she intoned sweetly.

"You guys reek of testosterone," Jewel said.

"What did you say to that guy?" I asked.

"I asked him why he was hitting on me," Ann answered. "When he had such tiny hands."

"After that it kinda went downhill," Jewel added.

Ann gave a cowboy holler that turned cowboy heads at the Silver Hill bar.

"What do you say, Buster?" Cheryl said. "Had enough stag party for one night?"

Buster put his arm around Cheryl. "For this wedding at least."

Outside the Silver Hill Inn, the moon shone clear in the thin mountain air.

"I drove over by myself," Jewel said to me. "Want a ride home?"

I climbed aboard and we took off. She drove in silence while the Ford's headlights poked at the darkness. A high-altitude chill put the edge to my growing sobriety. I braced my feet against Jewel's floorboards and jammed my hands into my jeans pockets.

"What was that all about?" I asked out of the darkness.

"Just another night out on the town," she said. "Montgomery style. Like it?"

"I thought the whole thing was weird," I said.

"What part? Us crashing the party?"

"No, no. That was cool. I'm talkin' about the guy that was hitting on you," I said. "He said some pretty weird things."

"We said some pretty 'weird' things right back at him." She giggled.

"That's not what I mean," I said.

"Okay," Jewel said. "I'll bite. Whassup?"

"I mean, like, the way he trashed Montgomery." I looked at the moon shining silver through the aspens. "What does he care?"

"Relax," she said. "He was just looking to get back at us for givin' him the business."

"Maybe. I thought he had it out for our crappy little mining town."

"Oh," Jewel said. "So now it's our crappy little mining town. We're making progress."

We reached my cabin at the bottom of town. Jewel pulled over, her dark, red hair falling down her back in a rich, thick braid.

"Thanks for the ride." I climbed out of the truck.

The dogs raced down the hill, barked once apiece, and began sniffing Jewel's truck. Zoom added his signature to the right front tires.

I stuck my head back in the cab. "I just wanted to tell you . . ."

"Uh huh . . ." Jewel cocked her head and waited.

"I can understand why that guy was hitting on you girls . . ."

"I'm sure you can." She turned off the Ford. "I'm comin' in."

I backed away from the door of the truck. Another voice that sounded like mine said, "I'll make coffee."

"Suit yourself, sailor," Jewel said. "I still got a buzz on and I'm keeping it."

I opened the door and — while Wooly and Zoom barked, panted, and nuzzled her in all the right places — she surveyed my barren little cabin. "You're traveling light, aren't you?"

"You got nothin', you got nothin' do lose." I stoked the fire and put the water up. "Bob Dylan said that."

"He also said 'don't think twice, it's all right,' " She lit one of my kerosene lamps and blew out the match.

I handed her the pint of brandy I kept on the kitchen counter.

She took a swig and started to whisper sing. "Ain't no use, sit and wonder why babe . . ." swaying over the floorboards. "If you don't know by now . . ."

I coiled up like the spring in a toy locomotive. *Flight impulse?* I thought. *Now? Don't be ridiculous.*

"Ain't no use to sit and wonder why, babe . . ."

I stood still while she circled me, hands shoved in her pockets.

"It'll never do somehow."

The pine in the firebox popped and burst into flame, the warm light shining through the rings on the stove top, casting shadows against the high-ceilinged room. She danced until she was standing before me. "When the rooster crows at the break of dawn . . . " Her breasts touched me lightly through my shirt. "Look out your window, I'll be gone." Jewel leaned forward and brushed her lips against mine. She smelled of soap, wood smoke, and brandy. She put my face between her warm palms, kissed me full on the lips, and I flew straight up the chimney and into the cold night air, singing to the stars in the sky.

COLORADO DYNAMITE

I woke up hung over but still tingling from my stag party dessert with Jewel. Back in California, Katie was holding down a fortress against my enemies. I struggled with my sense of responsibility but remembered her angry sign-off over the phone and her rusty-nail breakfast. Even before I left, Katie and I had not danced well together in months. I missed the kids more than Katie and was glad for my furry, porcupine-addicted comrades. Besides, Jewel had smelled so delicious, felt so warm. I let her pull me away from the past. In the present, I lay naked on my cold pallet, my head ached and Wooly and Zoom smacked the door with their tails and whined. They needed their dog chow. I needed coffee, pancakes, eggs.

A green Ford Bronco rolled down the road from the café. It sported a whip antenna and a red light on top of the cab. The Bronco slowed and stopped. A lean, crew-cutted man with a weathered jaw squinted at me.

"How's it goin' there?" Marshal LaPorte extended a hand.

I thought I'd grabbed a work glove. No, it was his hand, tough as leather.

"I'm Johnny LaPorte, the town marshal. Been meanin' to drop in, say hello, but they got me runnin' down at the job."

"Uh. Thanks. Pleased to meet you." I wasn't used to chit-chatting with the law.

"You gettin' settled into Hazel's place?" He eyed my cabin behind us. "Needs a little work, but it's a solid little place, right enough." He laughed. "Can't say the same for that wreck of a building she's got up in the middle of town. I hear she's got you goin' at that."

"Yessir. Looks like we're gonna rebuild it," I replied. The radio spurted cop talk.

"Well, good luck," he said. "You must have charmed old Hazel. She's usually tight-fisted as all get out."

"Well I . . ."

"Look, here, Gus. Welcome to Montgomery. I gotta run. Just wanted to say hello." He put the Bronco in gear. "If you're headed up to the café, don't be surprised. You're getting more than your fair share of the law today." He laughed at my confusion. "No big deal," he said. "Just don't let the bastards get ya down." Marshal Johnny LaPorte rolled away down the canyon road, giving me a whoop with his siren.

I found Reisinger sitting at the counter in Ed's café, soaking up caffeine. Juicy Brucie was leaning over a café booth, jawing with two uniformed Boulder County deputies. I slid onto a stool and Ed poured me a cup of coffee. "How long has the heat been here?" I asked.

Ed shrugged. "Never seen county pigs in here before."

"Your marshal stopped me on the way up . . ."

"Ah. So you met Johnny LaPorte," Ed said.

"Don't worry about it," Reisinger said. "He's one of us."

"He told me they were up here," I said. "Sounded like a warning."

"Trippy," Reisinger added. "Boulder County pigs. They usually hang out with the rednecks in Silver Hill."

"And what's he doing?" I jerked a thumb in Brucie's direction. After his trouble-making caper at the stag party, I didn't like him and I didn't trust him. "Kissing ass?"

Reisinger turned to look.

Laughter subsided from the booth where the two deputies sat. Brucie pushed away from the lawmen, crossed to the big pot belly stove and warmed his hands.

"It isn't lit, Brucie," Reisinger said. "You cold?"

"No," Brucie replied. "I was just thinking. You got any extra stovepipe?" Brucie asked.

"What for?" Reisinger asked.

"I'm putting in a new stove."

"Where you getting it?" Ed asked. Along with pickup trucks, stoves were a high-priority topic in Montgomery.

"You got cash to buy a new stove?" Reisinger asked.

"Sure," Brucie said.

"Brucie." I leaned past Reisinger. "Where do you get your money?"

"I run a business." Brucie sounded tight. "Imports. Sweaters, hats. I was in the Peace Corps down in Peru."

"So you made a few deals on the side?"

"Yeah, sure," he said. "In the city. Lima. Real nice people. You'd never know they were Indians." He leaned away from the counter, wanting to leave.

"So . . ." Reisinger grabbed Brucie's sleeve. "So you got Peruvians knitting sweaters and hats for you."

"I can get the stuff real cheap."

"I bet you can." I slurped my coffee. "And sell it real expensive.

Brucie didn't catch the contempt. "Down in Boulder," he said. "They eat that native stuff for breakfast."

"I bet they do," Reisinger said.

Brucie's under-the-table Peace Corps deals had gotten to Reisinger. I didn't blame him. Peace Corps profiteer. Rip-off artist. He wasn't the first. Talking to this guy made me feel like I needed to wash up.

The two sheriffs rose out of their booth, guns and radios thumping.

"Scuse me." The voice told me the person didn't care whether he was excused or not.

I turned around. One of the officers was out on the porch picking his teeth but the other one — a bow-legged trooper with a big belly and a sour mouth — focused straight down on me. One hand rested on the back of my stool, the other hung near his gun.

Outside, a radio squawked from the Blazer. He ignored it.

"You talking to me?"

"You new around here?"

The other officer squinted back through Ed's screen door. "Let's go, Rowdy."

Rowdy, I thought. *Perfect.* I wasn't up for a chat with any Boulder County Sheriff, particularly one named Rowdy. Reisinger sipped his coffee, shoulders up around his neck.

Brucie helped himself to a piece of pie from the counter and began to eat with his fingers, a look of cross-eyed concentration on his face.

"Where you from?" the deputy asked.

I heard the screen door screech. The other deputy stepped back inside.

I turned around to face my tormentors. "California." The guy looked familiar.

"You have any identification on your person?"

"Nope." I just couldn't squeeze out a 'sorry, sir.'

"You operate a motor vehicle without a license?"

"I got a license." Damn. I was already slipping. I had violated the first rule of the resistance — keep your papers in order. "It's just down at my place is all."

"Don't do you a helluva lotta good down there now, does it?"

I didn't want him to know where I lived, either. Double damn.

The other deputy stood by the café door, covering us criminals at the counter.

"How 'bout your draft card. Where's that at?"

"Down the house, with the rest of my stuff." In his cop suit, I just couldn't place the guy. But where had I seen him?

"You're supposed to carry that card on your person at all times." He sounded as if he was reading from a manual.

"I never been asked for my draft card before," I said. "Isn't that a job for the feds?"

The deputy loomed over me like a galoot in a bad western. The smell of coffee and Marlboros slithered out from under his mustache. "Draft dodgers is everybody's business," he said. "You look strong enough to fight for your country. What's your problem? You got a disease or somethin'?"

"I got a One - Oh," I told the deputies.

"What did you say?" The deputy pushed his belly in my face.

"A 1 - O. One oh. I'm a conscientious objector." I looked straight into the buttons on the sheriff's shirt. "I don't believe in war."

"You don't believe in war." He turned to his partner. "You hear that, Roy? He don't believe in war." He turned back. The leather on his gun belt make a squeaking sound. "You too good to fight?"

"I don't think people should kill people."

"So . . ." he said. "I don't want to fight, all I gotta do is sign up for one of your coward's licenses?"

"Conscientious objector's status. As defined by the Selective Service administration. You have a right to plead your case on religious or moral grounds. They decide."

The deputy turned to his partner. "I like that, don't you, Roy? All we got to do is say we don't want to fight for our country and bingo! We're home free. Let them other jokers fight."

"And die," Roy added.

"You musta done something right," I said.

"What's that supposed to mean?" pot belly snarled.

"You're standing here safe and sound, aren't ya?"

Reisinger groaned out loud.

Rowdy grabbed me by the shirt front, whisked me off my stool, dragged me through the clattering screen door, and smacked me up against the black and white Blazer.

"Listen, California," he hissed. "We know you ain't all about peace and love. Not with them people blowing up high tension lines out there."

What was this guy talking about?

"What people?" I asked. "Where?"

"Shut up, you little freak. As if you didn't know." He tightened his grip on my shirt front. "They're usin' Colorado dynamite. If we find out that you — or anybody else around here — is smugglin' illicit explosives across state lines, you're going to be sorry you ever dragged your cowardly commie ass out of hippieland." He slammed me against the Blazer one more time for emphasis. "Let's get out of here, Roy," he said. "The smell is startin' to make me sick."

Rowdy and Roy slipped into the Blazer. Rowdy leaned out the window. "I got my eyes on you, California." I watched the lawman duo bounce downhill and disappear around the bend. That's when I remembered him. He had been at the Silver Hill Inn last night, mixing it up with the cowboys. "Small world," I muttered.

Reisinger and Brucie stood frozen at the doorway of the café, leaving me alone to wonder. . .*Who had been talking to the Boulder County Sheriff's department about Colorado dynamite, California power poles, and sabotage? And about me?*

The One-Lunged Miner

"Hey, look what I found!" Sullivan knelt in the debris of Hazel's partially demolished building. A tight coil of tens and twenties exploded out of his fist and fell on the floor. Dust rose into the sunlight.

"Holy shit," said Reisinger.

"Where did that come from?" I asked.

"I was bustin' out that wall and clang! This damned thing hit me on the head." Sullivan held up a rusted baking powder can with a faded Indian head logo. His crowbar lay on a pile of splintered planks. "We're rich!" he shouted, eyes flashing behind his bushy head of hair. "Fuckin' rich!"

I had hired Sullivan and Reisinger to help me with Hazel's building. They both signed on happily. Prior to the founding of the Gus 'n Hazel Construction Company, the only jobs in town were at Ed's Peak-to-Peak Café or up at a silver mine on the Eldora road.

Eldora was an abandoned mining town built within shotgun range of the Continental Divide. The mine was called the Buckshot in deference to the wind that blasted the barren ridge top where the mine's solitary head frame sat. In the winter, miners went to work in the dark, toiled all day in the mine, and returned to the boarding houses underground without seeing sunlight – except for Sundays.

Eldora had been wiped out by diphtheria three times since it was founded in the 1880s. The only remnants of the town were the foundations for the whorehouse and the brewery, both constructed with good Welsh stonework, indicating the priorities of a society where men worked underground, ate nothing but canned beef and potatoes for months on end, sewed themselves into their underwear in November and slept alone in boarding houses wallpapered with the *Leadville Gazette*.

The abandoned Buckshot mine had been recently bought by a clairvoyant named Arthur Sigismunde, who was convinced that the old diggings still contained silver. It was possible. Work on the Buckshot had come to an abrupt halt in the 1950s after the two owners had gotten into an argument. While one partner drove his truck down to Denver to talk to his lawyer, the second partner drank himself nasty and lowered a bucket of dynamite with a lit fuse halfway down the vertical mine shaft. The resulting concussion sent splintered mine timbers, copper wire, galvanized pipe and a cascade of gravel, granite, and mud spilling hundreds of feet down the shaft where the whole mess fused into a massive plug that blocked access to the ore below.

In an alleged fit of extrasensory clarity, Sigismonde had visualized masses of rich, silver ore pulsating below the plug. He managed to convince a clique of Denver entrepreneurs, men who could smell the romance of silver in the mountains and had money to spend. Sigismonde avoided hiring high-waged miners who belonged to the United Mine Workers. Instead, he hired Norman Bowkers and Eddie Williams to run the operation.

Eddie was considered a genuine character in the fringes of Boulder's academic aristocracy. Although he came on as an simplistic mountain man full of country ways and independent views, Boulder's tiny cadre of literati marveled at Eddie's "natural" intelligence and unpretentious, cut-to-the-chase style. He and Sigismonde had drifted through many a notable conversation at Boulder parties and Eddie had done a stint as a hard rock miner somewhere in his enigmatic past. So authentic did he appear, that few knew he had been disinherited as the black-sheep son of a Boulder professor emeritus.

With Eddie in charge of the Buckshot mine, Montgomery had an inside line on jobs at the mine. Everybody was eager to work. There wasn't much cash to be had in the mountains. Eddie and Norman immediately engaged a handful other hippies from Montgomery. The amateur miners were supposed to retimber the mine and untangle the mass of dynamited debris that hung, suspended precariously 800 feet above the bottom of the Buckshot's shaft. Eddie, Norman, and the others were literally dismantling the floor they stood on.

Besides being dark and dangerous, the work was spotty: Sigismunde's aspirations often outstripped his patron's generosity, forcing him to halt operations while he raised more money. During the down time, Sullivan and Reisinger had been glad to stay in town and work for Hazel and me. The job was steady and sunlit and I had promised to pay cash every Friday.

Now, Reisinger had dropped to one knee and scooped the greenbacks off Hazel's floor.

Sullivan grabbed it back. "Gimme that," he growled. "I found it."

"That was quick," Reisinger said. "From 'we're rich' to 'gimme' in a flash."

Sullivan made it to $600 before I put a hand on his wrist. "This is Hazel's building," I said.

"Oh, camaaahn," groaned Sullivan. "What about the laws of salvage?"

"We're not at sea, Sullivan," I said. "It's Hazel's money."

"What a fuckin' goodie-two-shoes," Sullivan growled.

"You might say we liberated the bread," Reisinger said. "She doesn't need it, Gus. She owns half the town."

"Hey, you two geniuses," I put in. "Maybe you can figure this out for yourselves. How fast does word get around this town?"

"Not between us and her," Sullivan said. "She's an old lady, man. She don't know what's happening."

"I wouldn't put money on that," Reisinger added. "Still, it doesn't have to go any further than us. I could sure use the bread."

"Look," I said. "She'll probably turn it around and put it back into the building."

"Oh wow," said Sullivan. "That's great. Maybe she'll buy us a six pack of Bud."

"Yeah," I said. "And maybe she'll buy a stove for the basement so one winter day, when you're freezing your ass off, you can pull your truck inside and work in the warmth and comfort of your local community garage."

"Don't give me that shit," Reisinger warned. "You can't eat utopia. Baby needs a new pair of shoes."

"You got your nose too far up the old lady's ass," Sullivan sneered.

"Gimme the money, Sullivan," I said.

Sullivan growled.

Wooly looked up from his paws on the floor. A lip curled back over his canines.

I don't like to fight. I avoid it whenever possible, which is most of the time. I certainly didn't want a two-against-one with these guys and I didn't think Wooly or Zoom would be much help. I looked around. There were plenty of ways to get nasty. The floor of the half-demolished building was littered with debris. Sullivan's crowbar and a framing hammer lay within grabbing range. I wasn't about to take up arms against my brothers, but I couldn't be sure they wouldn't.

Slowly, Reisinger rose up off his knees and wiped his hands on his jeans. Zoom growled and got to his feet. Reisinger picked at a splinter in his palm, ignoring the dogs.

Silence.

No one moved.

"Fuck you, man." Sullivan threw the money on the floor, pushed himself up from his knees and walked down the wobbling, two-by-ten gangplank.

Reisinger resumed picking at the horny hide of his palm.

"I can't hold out on the old lady," I said.

"Shit, man," Reisinger replied. "Do what you gotta do. I'm gonna take the rest of the day off." He picked up his tool belt and lumbered down the gangplank. "I coulda used the money," he repeated and followed Sullivan up the road, leaving me standing alone in the ruins of Hazel's half-wrecked building, a roll of money in my hand.

I twisted the cash into a roll and tried to stuff it back in the baking powder can. The coil wouldn't fit. Whoever stashed the bread had jammed bills into the can until there was no more room. I climbed into the truck, rolled the cash into the glove compartment, and backed our days' work — a load of salvaged lumber — across the road to the Odd Fellows' Hall.

After I had tossed the splintery planks onto the floor of the cavernous old building, I clambered inside and began sorting and stacking the recycled lumber. My thoughts came with the rhythm of my movements. If we were liberating money for the collective good, that would have been okay. But Sullivan and Reisinger wanted the money for themselves. I imagined Hazel might put the money back into the building. I wanted to believe that. But no matter, I wasn't going to take candy from an old lady.

When I finished sorting the lumber, I pulled off my gloves and sat for a moment in the cool darkness of the deserted hall. Framed by the doorway, the hillside across the canyon shimmered green and golden in the heat. Sullivan's truck flashed past, headed down the canyon. His middle finger extended from an upraised fist. I sat in the darkness, studying my stained and splintered hands. A breeze stirred the aspens outside. The building sighed and shifted.

I heard the sound of chair legs scraping the floor above, as if a person was pushing away from a table. I froze.

A shot of adrenaline coursed through my body and the hair prickled on my arms. All I could hear was the sound of the mountain crickets, the wind, and the patient creak of the old structure as it adjusted to the gentle pressure of the wind.

I heard a cough, a single hack. I rose, doubting my ears. The hack multiplied into a string of wet convulsions as the cougher worked up a ball of phlegm and spat it on the floor.

"Anybody up there?"

No reply. I was talking to the wind and the crickets. I tiptoed to the foot of the stairs and listened again. A faint wheezing floated down the stairwell like the uneven rasp of a sleeper. I put my foot on the lowest step and stopped, waiting for a reaction, a word from upstairs. The silence of decades rang in my ears. I began the long climb up the staircase. It clung precariously to the back wall. The treads and risers creaked and protested, unused to the weight of a human body. I stopped halfway up.

"How'd you get up there?"

I heard the feathery whistle of breath and continued my climb. I pictured the stairway collapsing straight down in a screech of groaning timbers and a cloud of dust. I reached the top and stopped again. Sunlight blared through a single, dust-encrusted window at the end of the room. As my eyes adjusted, I could make out a clutter of circular tables and bentwood chairs tumbled across the floor.

The window threw a square of dusty light onto the floor. Just beyond the square, a man sat in a bentwood chair, chest collapsed, elbows perched on chair arms supporting his fragile frame. He was thin and gray-haired with a grizzle of beard. A spiky, self-inflicted haircut flared like a halo against the backlight of the window.

"How's it goin'?" I asked.

"'Bout frickin' time you got up here." He had a voice like a punctured accordion. "Between you and them other two bozos, you make enough noise to wake the dead." He hawked another lunger at the floor. "Who the hell are you, anyways?"

"Name's Gus," I said, moving toward him, hand extended. "Gus Bessemer."

"Just stay right there, Beelzebub."

"Bessemer."

"Whatever you like. This floor's full of potholes. I wouldn't want to bet on which of these frickin' joists'll hold and which won't. Best be cautious of timbers, above ground or below," he wheezed.

"Timbers." I recognized the term from hearing Eddie Warren and Norman talking about work at the Buckshot mine. "You a miner?"

The old man held up a two-fingered claw, all that remained of his left hand. "Minin' took the rest," he said. "And my right lung to boot. Don't have shit or shinola to show for it, neither," he added as an afterthought. The old man cocked an eye at me and said, "You're no frickin' rockhound are you, boy?"

I shook my head.

"What the hell you doin' down there, anyhow? You people're wreckin' the whole goddamned town." He snorted to himself. "Might as well. Nobody'd miss it," he added in a tone that smoldered like battery acid. "Frickin' place is gone to the dogs."

"And you are. . ." I said.

"None of your good goddam business us who I am. I been here since nineteen and forty-eight. On and off. Couldn't stand the place more 'n a year at a time. Price of gold was up then. Made it worth while, livin' up here. Nowadays I get out for the winter. Goddamn cold cuts my lung like a frickin' knife. Nobody in their right mind stays here in the winter. Only way it's worth it? Gold. Rest of you people are crazy."

"So what are you doing up here?" I asked. "Beside watching me?"

"That's none of your goddamned business, neither, Beelzebub," he replied.

"It's Bessemer."

"Never mind that," he said. "Somethin' you gotta know. . ." He coughed once, then wheezed. Alarm filled his rheumy eyes as he gasped for breath and hacked out a chain of convulsions.

I made a move toward him but he stopped me with a single move of his skinny arm, palm held perpendicular. The cough climaxed with a phlegm-filled cadenza that spewed a second goober on the floor.

"Don't get all bent outta shape. It ain't tuberculosis," he wheezed. "Silicosis. From drillin' dry. It's against the law now, but back in the old days, you did what you had to. Anything to get the frickin' ore out. Boss or no boss, you did what you had to. But I didn't call you up here to bellyache about my health."

"You didn't call me up here at all. Did you?"

The old man ignored my question. "This town is sittin' on the edge of a precipice. You don't want to be around when the wind starts to blow. Things get crazy around here. The whole frickin' place is liable to blow right over the frickin' edge. There. That's all I got to say."

"Look," I said. "Who told you that I. . ."

"Don't start with any of your frickin' crybaby questions. I don't want any part of it. But don't say I didn't warn you. This place deserves everything it gets. Borne and bred by greed, raised on hard work and misery."

"You don't have much of an opinion of the place," I said.

"Prob'ly don't seem so bad at first. You'll see. Things've changed. The lawful and the lawless, runnin' hand in hand. You'll see, if you ain't figured it out already." He began to cough again.

"What'd you mean, 'the lawful and the lawless?'"

"Who said that?"

"You did, just now," I replied.

The old man shifted impatiently in his chair. "You think I remember everything I say? Now get out of here," he hissed and pointed to the stairway with his claw of a hand.

I turned to go and the old buzzard grabbed my shirt sleeve. I could feel the tremors of age tugging at my forearm.

"Name's Matthews," he said. "Carl Matthews. You don't need to go blabberin' it all over town. Just so's you know." A lightning bolt flashed bright-white against the window, followed by the crack and rattle of its passage. Carl Matthews looked like he was going to cackle once or twice and fly out the window like a bat.

I nodded and light-footed it down the stairs. Another paroxysm of silicosis, the chair scraped on the floor, and I leapt off the loading dock into the roadside dust. I took a deep breath to get the dust and shadows of the Odd Fellows' Hall out of my lungs. A thunderhead had reared up over the ridge tops and turned the sunlight to gray and black. I climbed into my truck just as the first rain hit. I was rattled. First that hassle with Sullivan and now this weird, unheralded conference with a one-lunged miner named Carl Matthews.

Wooly and Zoom leapt into the back of the truck to get out of the rain.

"What the hell, guys." I tried to sound casual. "No more wrecking ball today. Might as well go down to Hazel's and unload the money." I trundled down Left-Hand Canyon Road and slithered across the plank bridge that crossed the creek to Hazel's. I opened the glove compartment.

The money was missing.

I put the truck in reverse and backed away from Hazel's. I didn't want to stumble through this scenario with Reisinger and Sullivan and a roll of missing money until I figured out what happened.

I drove slowly uphill in the rain. Reisinger didn't seem like a thief. Sullivan was a likely candidate but he had driven down the canyon while I was in the Odd Fellows Hall. My steel trap mind told me that Reisinger wouldn't know that Sullivan had stolen the money. He was likely to gab about the whole episode and my confiscation of the funds. Sullivan wouldn't brag about the money, not if he had stolen it. I'll just sit around the café and nurse a beer, I thought. Until somebody slips up.

I stopped.

I had come up here to get away from it all, work with my hands, simplify my life, say hello to my soul. Weeks later, I was already hip-deep in hassles and none of them of my making. But just because these hassles came to me didn't mean I could turn my back on them. *Or could I?*

"Fuck it." I turned off at my own cabin driveway. Tomorrow was Sunday. I'd spend the day sitting on my front porch, play my guitar, throw the *I Ching*, read Thoreau. I was determined not to leap from my recent past into whatever conflagration Montgomery, Colorado had lit under its own craggy butt.

I started a fire, poured beans into a pan, gobbed them with molasses and put a skillet full of cornbread in the oven.

Wooly and Zoom stared up at me, panting happily with their persistent, simple-minded agenda. I dragged out the food sack, heaped up their bowls, poured bacon grease over the top of everything and sat down with a beer to listen to the sound of the firewood popping in the stove. I watched my two mutts slurping up bowls of doggy grits and waited for the cares of the day to slip away.

TEEPEE PEOPLE

The cares of the day did not slip away. I couldn't get Hazel's missing cash out of my mind. And what about the crabby old guy who had materialized in the loft of the Odd Fellows' Hall? What was up with him? I left the dogs sighing on the cabin floor and walked up to the café. Jewel waved from behind the counter, Buster and Norman hunched over coffee mugs. Silhouetted by the bright day outside, Cheryl swept yesterday's rain off the back porch. Sullivan was noticeably missing.

I sat down next to Buster and Norman.

Jewel slipped me a mug of black coffee. "Almost noon," she said. "And it's Sunday. You guys ready to switch to beer?" Without waiting for answer, she pulled two Budweisers out of the cooler. She grinned. "Now Gus, he's sticking with coffee."

"And he looks serious," Cheryl said.

I laughed. I didn't want to come across paranoid about the missing money. Instead I tackled the mystery man. "Who's this crusty old guy, hangs out at the Odd Fellows' Hall?" I asked. "Has a couple of fingers missing, wheezes like a busted accordion."

Norman stared at me.

Buster stared at Norman.

"Boys," Jewel chimed in. "Help the man out."

"Carl Matthews," Norman replied.

"He's only got one lung," I continued. "He said something about silicosis and 'drilling dry.' What's that mean?"

"Drillin' holes for charges in hard rock," Norman explained. "Dry rock dust cuts your lungs to shreds. The drill bits have to be cooled by water. Lotta times, there wasn't no water. Old Carl couldn't breathe."

"Oh, cool," Cheryl said. "The good old days."

"So where'd you come across this Matthews guy?" Buster asked.

"I was unloading a stack of siding into the Odd Fellows' Hall. Just before yesterday's storm hit. I heard somebody coughing and spitting, went upstairs to check it out, and this guy was sitting by the window."

"Well, that's amazing," Norman said, looking at the people around him, rather than me. "Pretty damned amazing."

"Meaning . . ." I asked.

"Wow." Jewel pushed through the screen door and stood on the porch. She shielded her eyes. "Look what's coming down the mountain."

Norman, Buster and I followed her out. Cheryl joined us.

A school bus wound down the road from the Peak to Peak Highway. On its front, back and sides, psychedelic swirls morphed into wilderness landscapes, blue sky, white clouds, and noble savages on horseback. On top of the bus, a roof rack made of plumbing pipe, elbows, and t-joints supported the tightly bound poles and canvas of a dismantled teepee.

"Cowabunga," Buster said. "Injuns."

I bet myself that there wasn't an "injun" in the bunch.

The vehicle ground past Ed's café and parked in a corner of the lot, as far from the tourist vehicles as they could. The door popped open and a woman in a long paisley skirt and a tie-dyed tank top leapt down the steps and ran toward us. Her dark hair was parted into two braids, her arms circled by a myriad of silver bracelets that jingled as she came closer. On her feet were soft-soled boots of red suede leather.

"Who-ee," said Norman. "A damsel in distress."

The damsel hit the porch out of breath, leaned on the rail and panted, "We need help." Her brown eyes were rich and deep. "We've got a little girl in the bus. She's been hurt. Raped."

The tight little Montgomery posse crowded around her. The dogs broke into a barking cacophony.

"No, no," she said. "Don't make a fuss. She'll freak out."

"Sounds like you need the cops," said Buster, standing up to take control.

The woman in braids shook her head violently. "This little girl. She's not one of us and she . . ."

"Better get her to a doctor," Norman warned.

"You mind if I come over. Take a look at her?" Cheryl asked. "I was a medic."

We walked in a knot towards the bus. The dark-eyed woman stopped us at the door. The bus was dark and still. A figurehead sat frozen at the wheel, staring straight ahead through the windshield.

"My name is Georgia," the dark-eyed stranger whispered. "This little girl, we found her stumbling along the road this morning, just outside that town back there."

"You mean Holland?" Cheryl asked.

Holland was on the main road from Boulder to Estes Park. Bigger than Montgomery, Holland was flat broke and almost as ugly, a sad little cluster of winterized cabins, but it sported three bars, a gas station and a supermarket.

"This little girl. What did she say happened?" I asked.

"She met up with a buncha freaks," Georgia said. "She thought they were just another bunch of hippies. She's only fifteen, she was hitchhiking. They took her up in the

National Forest. She said at first it was all right, they were just partying."

"Whatever that means," Cheryl said.

Georgia continued. "Things got rough. By the time the night was over, the guys were taking turns fucking her while the others held her down and threatened to pull her teeth with a pair of pliers."

"She described these guys as hippies?" I asked.

"What kind of hippies would do that to a kid?" Jewel asked

War reverb, I thought. Violence redounds to the home front.

Georgia gave a thumbs up to the driver. The door opened to reveal a lean, shovel-bearded gatekeeper. He glared at us.

Georgia pulled Cheryl forward. "She's a doctor," she said. I caught judgment from the gatekeeper.

"No, I'm . . ."

Georgia kicked her silent.

The gatekeeper looked us over. "Those two . . ." He pointed to Buster and Norman. "Too big."

"Yeah," Jewel said. "Let's not overwhelm the poor kid."

"You," the gatekeeper pointed at my chest. "Come with your friend."

—

The guy was clearly in charge. I smelled cult. I'd seen it growing everywhere, from Boston to San Francisco. We climbed aboard.

A god's eye of rainbow yarn hung from the bus' broad rearview mirror. A fringe of prisms hung from the windows, shooting spikes of sunlight across a jumble of animal pelts and bird feathers, dried flowers and the skulls of owl, wolf, and badger. The air was filled with the smell of herb tea and incense.

Georgia led the way down a narrow aisle through a galley kitchen with a tiny sink, a two-burner stove, and a line of glass jars full of herbs, dried beans, and cereals.

Huddled into a bunk bed, a skinny, thin-haired teenager shivered under a blanket. A knot of the bus travelers gathered around her. They looked very young and very scared.

"Destiny, these people are here to help us," Georgia said. "They know how to get you to a doctor."

"No," blubbered the child, in a voice full of fear. "I don't want no doctor." She started to cry.

Destiny. What a name for this little unfortunate, I thought. She had bad teeth and a mid-Western accent. "Don't worry, honey," said Georgia. "We're not going to make you do anything you don't want to do."

"We know a place down in Boulder where you can get help for free," Cheryl added. "They won't ask you any questions, and they won't do anything to hurt you."

"No," the little girl whimpered.

Georgia leaned over her. "They'll just get you cleaned up, make sure you're all right."

I knelt down on the floor beside her and put my hand on her forehead. She was bright-eyed and feverish.

"It's my own fault," she said.

"No, it's not, honey," Georgia said. "Don't you ever think that. You didn't do anything wrong." Her voice was husky with tears.

"So, who were these guys?" Cheryl asked.

"I dunno," Destiny sniffled. "They wore pants covered with patches."

"Ah." Cheryl motioned us up front. The gatekeeper stood behind us, a tall lanky rag of a man with prominent teeth and a thick mane of hair. He wore an embroidered East Indian shirt beneath a vest adorned with pins and buttons.

"So who are the guys with the leather pants?" I asked.

"The STP Gang," Cheryl said. "They're 'way past pain in the ass. Things disappear when they come around. Last year they camped out in the National Forest between here and Holland and got badder by the week. I don't know where they go in the winter, but that patched-pants routine is a dead give-away. And those pants. They never wash 'em. The more patches you got, the bigger the honcho. Point of pride. They're disgusting."

"Not exactly love children," I said.

"Like Robin Hood on a bum trip," Cheryl added. "Steal from anybody and rub it all over yourself."

"Silly me." Georgia looked out over the horizon toward the foothills marching in gentle rows from shadow to sunlight. "I thought we were headed for paradise." She turned back to us. "That little girl needs a doctor."

"The free clinic down in Boulder," Cheryl said. "They'll look at her, for sure," she said.

"Where's it at?"

"Georgia, what are you saying?" the driver said. He had a French accent. "We don't have time."

I guessed that the Frenchman had a powerful agenda.

"Can one of you take her down?" he said. "We're full up."

"Michel." Georgia's eyes blazed.

"Look," French Michel said. "If we don't find a place to set up . . ."

"It can wait!" Georgia said.

Cheryl and I stayed out of it.

"We've already got more than we can care for." Michel jerked his head toward the quiet crowd at the back of the bus.

"Another one won't make a difference," Georgia said, her voice clipped.

"Trouble brings trouble," Michel said. "Look to the source. You don't know what vibe . . ."

"We're taking her to the city!" She ushered Cheryl and me down the steps. The bus door slammed shut. Georgia turned to Cheryl. Rage darkened her face.

No hippie, this chick, I thought. There's something happening here. Something else. Where was this Johnny LaPorte marshal guy when we needed him?

"Where's the clinic?" Georgia asked.

I guessed Georgia would handle Destiny's dilemma herself. She looked as if she could.

HIGH COUNTRY

Hazel's building was down. It was only the middle of August, but I could feel an edge on the mornings as I stacked the last of the useable lumber in the Odd Fellows' Hall. The thunderstorms of mid-summer had disappeared and the sky took on a brassy, polished look.

"Ice crystals," Norman and I were soaking up caffeine at the café. "I've seen it snow before the first of September."

Jewel, bar fights, porcupine quills, Hazel's building, stolen money, one-lunged miners and now, a gang of freaked-out acid marauders. No room to get my head together in this little mountain town. Maybe the truth lay higher up the hill, in the big peaks.

I packed a sleeping bag, a fishing line, a rucksack full of hiking grub and a bottle of brandy and drove into the National Forest above town. Norman had directed me to the trailhead of an old Arapahoe trade path that climbed through the high passes of the Continental Divide.

"You got to be crazy to wander around up there," Norman had said. "Air's too thin and a rock could fall on your head." He handed me a flask. "Here. Everybody's fool enough to roam around up there once or twice."

He stabbed a stubby finger at a blue emerald in the midst of the map's elevation marks. "Duck Lake," he said. "Good place to settle in for the night. Plenty of firewood scattered around and you might even catch yourself a fish or two for dinner." I climbed through the pines to the alpine meadows that soaked up the runoff from the snowfields above. I climbed beyond hunters territory into a prehistoric land. By noon I had reached the stunted pines around Duck Lake. The sun arched across the seamless bowl of a perfect sky. I clambered over granite moraines scrubbed by glaciers, threaded my way through talus slopes where boulders rested willy-nilly after crashing down from the great granite walls above. Each had broken loose, created a moment of thunder and then returned to stasis. Now, nothing moved. The chaos of stone surrounded me with silence.

I felt fear. Not of the exposure. I was smart enough to stay away from precipitous climbs. No. The fear came from the wilderness. A ringing, hissing, no-sound silence lay huge and hollow on the landscape, as if the vibrations of a great bell had rumbled down the canyon and fallen silent a million years before. Above me, the steep passes roared like dinosaurs. I was not the hunter, I was prey. Tiger bait like my ancestors, with millennia of rock and cave existence imprinting deep still pools of fear in my collective subconscious. But this primordial terror read like personal fear, my fear, mine alone to succumb to, mine alone to shake off, mine alone to ignore. I chose to live with it and carry on, regardless.

I snorted brandy to calm my nerves and made steady progress on switchbacks that cut across a barren rock face. By late afternoon I was above timberline. I had reached my limit. I was above 13,000 feet and still, the ragged, snow-capped massif flew up and away on either side like the granite wings of a great bat. I stopped. The sound of my breath was immense. It filled the void of the universe.

I looked back down toward the green-rimmed lake that would be my campsite. It glittered small in the bowl of tundra and glacial debris that fell away below me. I tried to imagine this same scene in the winter, the wind and snow whipping unchecked through these blasted canyons across the tundra to the pines below. The power of the place rolled over me, an ant, a speck, a nothing. At 14, 000 feet, I had been swallowed by the perfect madness of the wilderness.

A hell of a place for reflection, I thought. I barely existed here. How could I think? What plans could I make? Who down below, in that mountain town, who were my brothers and sisters? What had become of the enemy? I took a wad of money out of my pocket. The coins and crumpled bills lay abstract and meaningless in the callused crater of my hand. The wind blew the ball of a dollar away. I let it go and hunkered down on the barren granite slope.

Wind buffeted my eardrums. I was empty, a vessel bound by sinew, tendons, and the pulleys of my knees, ankles, elbows and wrists. I could hear my heart pound. I flexed my hand before my eyes and peered through my fingers. My spirit rushed out of my forehead, flowed through my fingers and dissipated into thin air.

I let go of the oil refinery that pounded flame into the sky. I misplaced the home I had shared with the tall, thin woman in jeans who smoked Camels and marked time, caring only for her two blonde children. I knew nothing of the grim logic pushing the crew-cutted, madras-shirted California boys into the Oakland Induction Center, or why I had pleaded so sincerely with them, or how a heavily armed U.S. destroyer in the Tonkin Gulf could have been threatened by a tiny typhoon-driven Vietnamese gunboat. I pondered the forces of war but they seemed blurred, the recollections of a drunk.

Five years earlier, my old man had driven me to a bus depot in a sad military town. I was headed to Philadelphia to join friends. They planned to repeat the voter registration efforts of the Mississippi Freedom Summer in the ghettos of the Northern industrial cities.

That day, he had been very anxious.

"Think you'll be going back to school?" he asked.

"I don't know."

"What about your room at the dorm? Will they save your room?"

"How do I know? I'm moving off-campus anyway," I growled.

"Why? How are you going to study if you live off campus?"

"Goddamit I don't know if I'm going back, never mind where the hell I'm gonna live or what I'm gonna study!"

Silence.

I stared out the window at the greenery. My face felt hot, flushed but inside, I felt cold, cruel. Of course I would go back to school, maybe not right away, but eventually. I held out on him. I had nothing to give.

We hit town. Main street revealed its desperate military dependence: faded officers' uniforms for sale in the store fronts, too many bars, and the deals for dogfaces in the used car lot. Tattoo parlors, lawyers' shingles, and photo shops offering quick pics for mom and the girl friend stared down from the second floor of the old brick buildings.

We pulled into the bus depot. I broke out of the passenger door like a prisoner released.

"Give me the keys," I demanded.

"What for?"

"The trunk!!! I gotta get my bag out."

"All right. Okay."

My old man turned off the engine and climbed out of the Plymouth. He trudged around the back of the car and fiddled with the trunk while I stood by, hands in my chinos. He pulled out the suitcase.

"There ya go," he offered.

I grabbed the suitcase out of his hands. He followed me into the bus station. Without looking back, I crossed to the ticket window. Through the bars, a scarecrow of an old Yankee peered at me through watery eyes.

"One for Philadelphia. One way."

My old man wandered over to the news stand. He began to push a revolving wire book rack around, checking its contents. The rack squeaked unevenly in the nearly empty terminal. He held up a paperback from the book rack. I turned back to claim my precious ticket and the change. Fourteen bucks to Philadelphia.

"You ever read this? *McTeague*?" His voice sounded thin and embarrassingly personal in the empty terminal. He crossed toward me holding up the book like a question mark, eyebrows raised.

The newsstand guy leaned out over his stack of Daily Records and Globes and hollered past the stub of a cigar. "Hey hey hey! You gonna buy that book, or just borrow it for a while?"

My old man jerked around like a puppet on a string. "Oh, yeah. Sure. How much is it?"

The newsie looked at him like he wasn't sure how this guy had reached middle age.

"Don't buy it, Pop. I don't need it," I said.

"It's written by the same guy who wrote *The Jungle*. Best piece of muck-raking ever written. That book led to the passage of the first pure food and drug acts." He handed the newsstand guy a dollar bill and me the book.

"You'll like it. Read it on the bus." The back of his hands looked like parchment. Something ached behind my eyes, something behind the anger and impatience.

"Thanks, Pop."

"Have a good time this summer." He studied a gum-speckled square of the bus station floor. "This Students for a Democratic Society. . .Why don't you join a labor union, you wanna organize people? That's the way to do it. Get 'em where they work."

"Thanks, Pop."

"Never mind. You'll probably learn something." The roar of a diesel pushed into the terminal. Beyond the dirty glare of the sun on the window, the silver and red mass of the Trailways bus glided into view.

"I gotta go now."

"Enjoy the book."

I jammed the book into my jacket pocket and clutched my belongings. My old man followed me to the door and stood there while I handed my suitcase to the driver. The driver's uniform bulged over a beer belly as he bent to stow it. I couldn't wait any longer. I climbed on board looking for a seat. Something made me stop. I turned.

The driver had navigated his girth past me into the driver's seat. I looked back down the steps at Johnny in his khaki pants and blue oxford cloth shirt.

"Thanks for the ride, Pop."

The newsstand guy came to the door and called out to Johnny, "Hey, mister. You want your change? You got it comin' y'know."

"Oh. Yeah. Sure."

My old man turned and walked back inside the bus station. I climbed the last step onto the bus. The doors closed, the diesel revved with a roar and a whine. Through the double-plated glare of bus window and bus station glass, I could see my old man talking to the newsstand guy. I had stuffed *McTeague* in my jacket pocket. That was the last time I saw him. He never said good-bye, not to me, anyway.

But then, I didn't say goodbye to him either.

Still high on altitude, I watched one of my crumpled dollar bills skip down the slope. I knew that my old man, his khaki pants and blue cotton shirt, his constant search for work, his sudden end, the money, I knew they were all connected. The People's Theater Collective, Montgomery, Colorado, the Blue Meanies and the draft board, they had come after the searing loss of my old man, but they were all linked. I just couldn't find the glue. I looked down at my hand. I could wiggle my fingers. I stood up, gained my equilibrium in the swirling heights, and began my descent.

By the time I reached the lake, the sun had dropped behind the ridges to the west. Mammoth shadows strode across the tundra. I found a sandy flat where I could dump my pack and spread my sleeping bag. I gathered deadwood snags for a fire and took a shot of Norman's brandy. In the reflection of the light cast down from the peaks, I pulled out the hand line, a number three hook, and the salmon eggs.

I found a pool where the water circled slow and deep and I could see the fish grazing, feeding off the algae that grew along the creek bank. The clever little bastards kept nibbling eggs off the hook, but if I gave a yank at just the right moment, I could haul them flopping onto the mossy tundra at the shoreline. I caught a little mess of the browns and cakewalked back to my campsite, grinning like a satisfied bobcat. I lit the snags, gutted the fish, and roasted them in one quick, chilled ritual. The cold came quickly with the setting sun. I half sung, half whistled a song I had learned ten years earlier, when I was still a kid.

> *Stayed around, played around,*
> *This old town too long,*
> *Summer's almost gone,*
> *Winter's comin' on . . .*

I gathered pitch-filled knots of the stunted, high-altitude pine that circled the lake, threw the knots on the fire, and spread my sleeping bag on the sand. I lay back against a log and drank the rest of the brandy before I fell asleep with the wilderness howling above my head. I dreamt no dreams. When I woke up, I knew that I was going to spend the winter in Montgomery, Colorado, hassles or no hassles.

TWO-SHIRT WEATHER

Two-shirt weather. That's what they called it. In the sunlight, you could work without a coat, but if you toiled in shadow or stopped moving, your hands and feet stiffened up. Pretty soon you were rubbing your palms together and stomping up and down in your boots. Two-shirt weather also meant you damned well better build up your woodpile before the windswept Eastern slope winter froze you.

The Saturday after I returned from the high country, a crowd of Montgomery's citizens drove up onto government land above town. In the interests of laying in a supply of firewood for the winter, a group of us had decided that six saws were better than one.

Flying on coffee and pancakes, a convoy of ancient pickups and flatbeds had left the café and climbed into the Roosevelt National Forest. We called it the King's Forest. I guess that made us Robin Hood and his merry band of men, only there was no Robin Hood in Montgomery, only freaks, anarchists, recluses, and draft dodgers. Besides half of Montgomery's merry men were women.

On that two-shirt Saturday, the whole town, or at least anyone who wanted to participate, roamed through the King's Forest, cutting, trimming, hauling, and stacking deadwood. Georgia and the Teepee People came along. They were happy to pitch in to secure firewood for their encampment. Even Eddie Warren, who usually kept to himself or disappeared down the mountain for days, contributed his pickup and sawed-off sinewy strength to the effort. If you didn't have a truck, if you didn't have a saw, no matter. Everybody worked, everybody got a share.

Deadwood was easy to spot. The silvery crags stood out, stark against the new growth around them. Standing deadwood dried slowly in the weather like the wicks of an exposed kerosene lamp. No water collected to soften the cellulose. Until they toppled onto the piney woods floor, they would not decay. Standing deadwood was hard and dry, easy to cut and split. It was perfect for cooking. After it was thrown on the fire, the tight grain of the high-altitude pine threw off the stored energy of the sun for hours.

That Saturday, we set up a wood-cutting assembly line. Three of us — armed with chain saws — marched through the forest spotting the big snags and cutting them down. An intoxicating aroma arose when the busy blades hit the crystallized pine pitch. A second wave of chainsaw-wielding citizens followed behind, cleaning the branches off the trunks and bucking the fallen timber into rough, eight-foot lengths that could be humped to the trucks parked in the clearing. Cold air, hot coffee, and whiskey kept us cutting and moving.

I worked ahead of the bucking crew, spotting and felling, inhaling the pine pitch as it rose into the clear air, watching colonies of black ants, sluggish from the cold, tumble out of the fallen spires that had been their metropolis. I had just knocked down a thick, straight snag about forty feet tall. With no foliage to cushion its fall, the dead log landed with a solid thump and the dry, sharp snap of breaking branches. High on destruction, I stepped over the fallen carcass, revving my chain saw, looking for another target. A thin, sweet stench hit my nostrils, penetrating the oily-hot smell of the idling saw. I stopped and my heart convulsed.

At the far end of the rotting trunk of an ancient Douglas fir, a human body lay face down, pigeon-toed, legs pronated inward from ankle to hip. I shut down the chain saw and stood, frozen in the warm sunlight. I didn't have to see the face. From the unnatural way the body curved to accommodate the terrain, I knew the spirit had left the frame. He couldn't have been long dead, this man, boyish hair tousled, arms tucked beneath his chest in awkward discomfort. Tenderness engulfed me. I wanted to take the lifeless form in my arms, to comfort its loneliness. Instead, I waited for my heartbeat to quiet so I could holler for help.

Reisinger was the first to arrive. Eddie Warren shut down his chain saw. Norman clambered over fallen logs looking skeptical. Buster and Cheryl came in from another direction. Juicy Brucie turned white as a sheet, said "Jesus," and looked away. No one moved. Jewel came looking to see where everybody had gone. In the distance, the sound of Malfese's chainsaw snarled its way through another standing dead snag.

Georgia burst into the clearing but held back. "Who is it?" she asked Jewel.

Norman took a breath, unclenched his hands, and walked gingerly along the backside of the fallen tree until he stood over the body. He bent over, stiff-kneed, hands on his thighs. He looked like an adolescent surveying a dead bird. Finally, he jumped to the ground, squinted at the body from another angle, then looked back at us.

"He's been shot," Norman announced. "In the back."

Eddie moved forward, hands thrust in his jeans, and gave the body a prod with his boot.

"Eddie, don't!" Cheryl said.

"Be good to know who it is." Eddie pushed harder and the body fell away from the fir snag and rolled face up. A hole the size of a grapefruit had been blown outward from its chest. Dried blood clotted the blues and purples of the corpse's plaid shirt.

Georgia let out a husky, full-throated scream which she broke quickly by thrusting both pitch-stained hands into her mouth. She collapsed to her knees, moaning, then curled into a fetal position on the ground.

"Jeez," said Reisinger. "Think she knows the guy?"

The little knot of woodcutters stood in awkward silence, watching her writhe on the sunlit pine needles. Buster kneeled next to her and touched her shoulder.

She tore his hand away.

Malfese broke into the clearing, still carrying his idling chainsaw. "Hey, am I the only guy cuttin' firewood up here? What's with you peo . . ." He stopped. "We got a problem?"

Georgia tried to approach the body a second time but could not. Instead she doubled over and broke into another chorus of incoherent sobs.

Reisinger returned with a square of canvas. We covered the broken body. Cheryl and Buster took Georgia back to Norman's truck, where there was another pint of Wild Turkey and a thermos of coffee.

"Who is this guy?" I asked.

"Ask Georgia," Buster said.

"I don't think she's gonna wanna do much talking just yet," Jewel said.

"We gotta tell somebody," said Reisinger. "We can't just leave him here."

"We can't move him," said Eddie. "He's been murdered."

"We gotta tell the authorities," Oriskany Bill said. It's funny. The guys who holler loudest about offing the pigs love to holler for help when the shit comes down. Oriskany Bill had just arrived in Montgomery in the back of a stake bed truck full of hippies and bedrolls. The hippies were headed for Boulder. Bill had hitched a ride somewhere in Utah and was on the run from the Navy after he dropped a foot-long machine bolt into the gear box of the Oriskany, an aircraft carrier bound for Vietnam. When the crew cast off and put the machine in motion, that bolt chewed through the transmission gears and the carrier ended up in dry dock. Before the authorities could shake down the crew, Bill was outta there. We all knew it because Bill had told us about it, first chance he got. For a guy on the run he had a big mouth and he sure did like to get noticed.

"The authorities, huh? Which ones?" Norman asked.

We better think about that," Norman said. "This town is already on the official shit list." Norman said.

"Yeah, but this is homicide," Reisinger said. "This guy didn't trip on his gun and shoot himself in the back," Reisinger said.

"But the county pigs?" Malfese said. "Puh-leeze."

"Besides, Georgia knows the guy," I said. "That raises the stakes. This horror show gives the county sheriffs an excuse to poke around anything up here."

"Shit." Norman regarded the lump of treated canvas. "We gotta tell Johnny. Before Boulder County gets wind of it."

"Last thing we need," Buster added, "is Johnny gettin' run over by the Boulder County Sheriffs."

The sober little crew worked its way back through the forest.

Cheryl stopped. "Y'know . . .The local coyotes aren't going to have much regard for states' evidence. For a coyote, that guy is just another blue plate special."

Wordlessly, we retraced our steps, rolled the cold, stiff body up in the canvas and hauled it down to the trucks.

I drove Georgia down the mountain. Brucie wanted to go along, but I didn't trust him. I wanted to be alone with her. I accused myself of taking advantage, but I was fascinated — by her connection to this guy and the circumstances of her heartbreak. I let the convoy of half-loaded trucks file past us and drove slowly downhill, waiting for her to talk, cry, or jump out the door.

"So, who is he, Georgia?"

"None of your business." She shook with sobs.

"I know this is a horrible time . . ."

"No, you don't!" She screamed like a child. "You have no idea."

"Yeah, I do." There was no use in explaining what my old man had done to himself. Or how it had made me feel.

"We've gotta know something about him, sister. Otherwise, we're all gonna get hit with a shit storm."

The trees flowed by on our descent while Georgia looked out the window. I had done the same, that day when my old man drove me to the bus station for the last time. Sudden death delivers commonality to its survivors.

"We were together. In California," she began, distant, eyes still turned away. "Before I came out here." In a voice flat with grief and fatigue, Georgia told me the story: This guy had been working with the Mobilization to End the War, the "Mobe," a powerful but conflict-ridden coalition that kept the nation's unruly, anarchistic, antiwar groups coordinated and connected.

"He wasn't one of the big politico mucky-mucks," Georgia said. "He wasn't a big talker. He operated behind the scenes, a get-the-job-done kind of a guy who had dropped out of school at Ann Arbor to fight the power." She sighed, a memory pushing the wind out of her. She turned to me. "You got a cigarette?"

I didn't.

"Jesus," she said, but continued. "He traveled all over the place, moving from campus to crash pad, making sure the hippies and students didn't fuck things up."

I knew the type. Indispensible. He made sure the permits were in order, that there was food for people, crappers at the demo sites, and that the medics got the training they needed to deal with the clubbed heads, torn ears, broken arms, and lacerated limbs. The grinding war and the troop escalation bore down hard on their lives.

For Georgia and this guy, their time together consisted of caffeinated, 72-hour organizing marathons and non-violence trainings followed by hastily-grabbed, exhausted flops on commune couches and no-budget, cross-country junkets. "He took it too personal," she explained. The Panther murders, the harassment and arrests, the sabotage of one underground newspaper after another, the discovery that the little freak down the hall was a snitch, the friends who got drafted and split for Canada. "He got quiet," she said. "Quiet and angry. He was beginning to mess me up. He never cracked. Never copped to how tired he was, or how scared he was, or anything. He was like a machine, like a Marine, like . . .one of them. He started to piss me off."

Georgia began to cry again. "I got to hate the sight of him. I didn't want him to touch me. When I knew it was going to get ruined, I told him we needed to change something. We needed to split. To mellow out," she said. "He wouldn't.

Looking at my own life now, living alone with two dogs in an old miner's shack and now, ankle-deep in the murder of a fellow traveler, I couldn't claim that mellowing out was a possibility. Anywhere. Georgia went on.

" 'We're nothing,' he'd say. 'You and me. What do our little problems mean, compared to the napalm and the nightmare over there?'" She stared out the window. "He tried to make me feel bad, but I wouldn't let him. I told him, if he burnt out, he wouldn't be any good to anybody. The Movement needs us,' that's all he would say. Over and over and over again. Shit."

"What was his name?" I asked.

She snapped around, fixing me in a wet-eyed stare. "Who wants to know?"

"I do."

"Why?"

"Just getting tired of calling him 'the dead guy.' "

"He's not 'the dead guy' to me."

"I'm sorry." She was already in enough pain. She didn't need me adding to it. "I don't need to know his name."

"It doesn't matter." She sighed. "Call him Joe."

"Okay," I said. "Joe."

She licked the tears off her upper lip like a kid. "He's gone now. But for me? He was long gone months ago. The Mobe needed him. It sure didn't need me. The guys made all the decisions. I was just Joe's old lady."

The way she tossed out his name told me that he really was Joe. Joe somebody.

"They took advantage of him. He did the work, they got the glory. I tried to point that out to him, but he just said 'it takes all kinds to make a revolution,' crap like that. I got disgusted. We went through the usual break-up bummers — threats, crying, all that pain and sadness. And now it all feels so . . .wasted."

I drove slowly, giving her time.

"But I didn't see where it was going. The war was getting more vicious, we were getting burnt out, going crazy. Finally, I didn't hear from him anymore." Georgia fell silent. She put her head on her knees, which she had drawn up on the seat beneath her long skirt. She smelled of pine needles and wet, salty flesh. I felt bad for her, but my head was full of questions.

What was this guy doing in a Rocky Mountain forest? Was he looking for her? Was he running away like me? Was it an accident, him wandering around the same mountains where his former girlfriend had landed with the Teepee People? I wanted to believe her story. This Joe guy, he could have been looking for her. Or, it could have been coincidence. Maybe he had another agenda. Something about dynamite.

It was impossible to know. The world was full of cosmic overlap, people splitting and coming together, crossing and re-crossing paths. These collisions weren't coincidental. They weren't accidents. We were traveling along lines not defined by any map, bonded by the effort to engage or avoid the enemy, to fight the system, to find a new way. Sometimes these collisions were weird or conflict-ridden, or — as in Georgia's case — tragic, but they were always significant. We considered every moment, every act as an affirmation of the size, range, and vitality of our community. We reveled in the belief that there were no coincidences, only the flow of one mind. Any moment could be significant. There was no order to it, only the mystery of the universe turned upside down by our own energy and the twin realities of war and the stinking, impotent karma of a nation that still believed its leaders.

It was dusk when Georgia and I got down the mountain to Montgomery. I headed directly for Johnny LaPorte's place. She didn't want to go but I wouldn't let her bail. Cosmically, politically, or passionately, she was connected to this dead Joe guy in the back of Norman's truck and — despite my wish to believe — I knew she was holding out.

LaPorte's home stood like a practical salute to mountain tranquility. The windows were tight, the trim glistened with fresh black enamel, the roof had been recently re-shingled, and a brand-new stove pipe jutted straight into the darkening sky. A silver propane tank squatted in the side yard like a beached submarine. Propane gas supplied all the comforts of flatland life to Johnny and his wife, Marie.

Norman and Malfese were already at Johnny's. The tarpaulin still covered the sad form, but the quarter-inch rope that had secured it against Norman's truck bed lay undone.

"Johnny must know the story by now," I said.

Georgia shuddered and looked away from the crumpled canvas in the truck bed. Johnny came to the front yard and fixed us with a stare. He was smoking a pipe. I had never seen him do that before. Silent, he motioned us inside.

A propane cook stove and enameled heaters percolated in every room, carefully surrounded at a safe distance by overstuffed furniture, layers of rugs and carpets, and a mountain of bric-a-brac. Marie rarely ventured out, and had arranged an intricate world for herself in the tiny dwelling. Doilies, memorial plates from coronations and inaugurations, photos of her son in Marine uniform, china dogs, and homey slogans littered every available surface with an order that probably only she could understand.

At home, Johnny looked even less like a lawman than he did in his Bronco. He had on a faded blue mechanic's shirt with a name tag that said "Johnny" sewn above the breast pocket. His worn service jacket was unzipped and he was unarmed.

He sat us down with Norman and the Monk and pointed his pipe at Georgia. "These fellas say you know this man," he said. "Is that true, honey?"

"I knew him."

"What's his name?"

"Joe."

"Joe what?"

She exhaled. "De Stephano. He was my boyfriend."

She wasn't letting go of any more than she had to. She shared the instinct we all carried in those days. Montgomery's folksy town marshal was still the Man. She and Joe had been living together in Oakland, California for two years before they broke up, she said. She had to get away so she went on the road with the Teepee People. Joe stayed behind. It wasn't the story she had told me, but I didn't say anything.

"Well," said Johnny. "We got a problem. You know I'm gonna have to turn the body over to the authorities down in Boulder. They're going to want to know what your connection is to the deceased, young lady."

Georgia nodded and bowed her head, eyes shut tight, like a kid who doesn't want to see the scary parts of a horror show. But I knew. Joe DeStephano wasn't a hippie. He was a left-wing radical. A big difference. She knew it, I knew it. Nobody else in this room knew what a difference that would make to this story.

"These other people that you come to town with. On your teepee bus. Any of them know this fella?"

"No," Georgia said. "They're not like him."

Powerful arcs of light swept out of the darkness. The door burst open and the room filled with the brown jackets and badges of the Boulder County Sheriff's Department. Two troopers stepped inside, guns drawn.

Johnny jumped to his feet.

"Siddown, everybody." There stood Rowdy and Roy, the same trooper duo from the Silver Hill battle who had rousted me at Ed's café.

Outside, two Boulder Sheriff's Blazers roared up the hill, headed for the café. The red strobe of a patrol car flashed through Johnny's window.

"What the Sam Hill d'you . . ." Johnny began, then thought better of it. His shoulders fell as he turned around, looking like he'd been double-crossed. His wife, Marie, stood in the parlor doorway, angry and confused.

"Anybody else on the premises?" Fat Rowdy motioned his partner to search the little house.

Johnny sat back down at the table. "Put your damn guns away and stop acting like fools."

"Shut up, LaPorte," the trooper replied. "Before I take the whole bunch in, you included."

"What's the charge?" Johnny asked.

"How about obstruction of justice? You got a dead body out there in the back of that truck. Why didn't you notify Boulder County?"

"Didn't have a good, goddamned chance." Johnny was cold, dead angry. It shone in his eyes.

"Here's your chance," the trooper said. "What do you know?"

"Not a blessed thing," Johnny snapped. "You guys stormed in here before I could find out diddly-squat. These people found the body up in the National Forest, shot-

141

gunned from back to front, went through the fuss to wrap it up in that tarpaulin out there, and drag it back down here. That's the long and short of it."

"We figured it was better to bring him down. Didn't want the critters to get him," Norman explained.

"Who asked you?" Rowdy turned back to Johnny. "You got all kinds of flag-burnin' commie friends up here, don't you, LaPorte?"

"Who told you boys about this fellah?" Johnny asked.

Police lights revolved on Blazer cabs, throwing red stains across Marie's homey kitchen walls. Outside, police radios spit and squawked in the cold air above the sound of idling V-8s.

"We're confiscatin' the body," Rowdy said. "After they do an autopsy, you can bet your butts we'll be back. I find out that any of this hippie-dippie, peace-and-love clan has moved a goddamned inch, I'm gonna start squawking conspiracy. That includes you too, LaPorte." The door slammed shut.

We sat still.

Outside, the sound of bundled canvas hissed off Norman's truck bed. Grunts, a thud, and sudden laughter shot through the door, followed by a chorus of low-pitched, raucous comments. Blazer doors slammed shut. The lawmen pulled away in convoy, red lights flashing in the cold dark air.

Johnny slapped the table with his open palm. "Lord love a duck," he muttered.

Georgia sat lonesome, hands folded, eyes closed.

Marie brought out a bottle of Wild Turkey and set it on the kitchen table.

Johnny poured a big shot into his coffee cup and swallowed the whole mess in one gulp. He looked around the room, fixing each of us in an angry stare. "All right," he drawled. "Which one of you idiots got on the phone with the sheriff's department?"

We all opened our mouths to object.

Johnny put up his hand. "You realize the pickle this puts me in? Havin' these guys barge in here while I got an unreported murder victim on my hands?"

"Camaahn, Johnny," Malfese said.

"We didn't tell nobody about this," Norman said. "We made our mind up in the forest. When we found the body and all — we was comin' to you."

Johnny began to pace his tiny kitchen floor. "Before them bozos busted through the door," Johnny said, "you guys wasn't here more'n ten, fifteen minutes with that stiff." He turned to Georgia. "Sorry."

She looked up at the low ceiling and blew the bangs off her face.

I wanted to put my arm around her. I did not.

"It takes those boys twenty-five or thirty minutes to haul their butts up here. That means somebody called Boulder County before you got here. "

"We couldn't have," Reisinger said. "Nearest phone's up at the café.

"Besides, we wouldn't bust your balls like that," Malfese interjected. "Honest to God."

"Who all was up there in the forest?" Johnny asked.

"Practically everybody," Norman said.

"Hell, it ain't my damned reputation I'm worried about," Johnny said. "But those people want to bust this place big time."

"We know that," I said. "But who? And why?"

"Big companies! I'm talkin' Raytheon, IBM, Hewlett-Packard. They all want to put brand new facilities down there on the prairie, right at the foot of the flatirons."

"What's that got to do with us?" Cheryl asked Johnny.

"They don't want any roving gangs of hippies or squatters messin' up the countryside, and they don't want crusty old-timers holdin' onto their land either. We're talking ski areas, campgrounds . . ."

"Up here? In Montgomery?" I asked, incredulous.

Johnny nodded. "We're standin' in the way of progress."

"That's progress?" Norman asked. "Buncha tourists?"

"Think about that," Johnny said. "Not tourists. Full-time, high-paid, tax-dollarin' wage earners and home buyers."

Norman rocked back, snapped his fingers and hee hee'd. "Got it," he said.

"So long as we keep this town runnin' proper, they can't touch us," Johnny said. "But if they break us down, we lose the town charter. Then they clear you people out and start panderin' to flatland weekenders and white-collar workers."

"They must be pissed," Cheryl said. "We got a lot of new people, we're putting up a new building, Ed's café is booming."

"I dunno," Johnny said and stopped long enough to pour another slug of bourbon into his cup. "But whoever it is . . .and whatever the reason, they sure know how to fuck with Montgomery, Colorado."

STAYED AROUND, PLAYED AROUND

By the time the wind began to blow, we had Hazel's new building framed out. The whole town chipped in to nail down flooring, slap sealer on the brand-new cinder-block foundation, or simply clean up scraps and sawdust. We hammered the weathered siding back. The rejuvenated one-by siding graced the front of the building with its weathered silver glow. We built roof trusses from a template chalked on the floor and slung them onto the top plate, nesting each truss neatly against the new-used ceiling joists.

That evening, Montgomery's notorious wind introduced itself, sprinting downhill in gusts, kicking up clouds of dust and levitating trash around the building site. At first, I didn't take any notice. I'd seen the wind blow before in Montgomery during thunder squalls. But this wind would be different.

The first sign of things to come happened, not on the mountaintops, but inside my cabin: I couldn't get the stove to draw. That puzzled me. Wooly and Zoom scratched at the door, whining to come in. That, too, was odd. I let them in, the wind nearly yanking the door from my grip, and stepped into the weather.

The frigid conflagration tore over the cabin tops like a witch on a broom. Trees bent evenly in the relentless blow, leaning away from the gale with a radical tilt. The air smelled of ice. Gusts smacked me on the shoulder and knocked me off-balance. There was no more dust in the air; it had blown clean away.

I scanned my roof in the whistling darkness. The wind was blowing across the chimney cap with such high-pressure velocity that the smoke could not escape. I thought about seeking shelter at the café, but figured I better keep a weather eye on the cabin and the dogs. Eventually, the chimney warmed enough to pull air through the firebox and across the smoldering coals. I got water to boil, baked up a crock full of macaroni and cheese, and drank myself silly, talking big to calm the dogs and listening to the storm lift up the corner of the cabin and slam it back onto its foundations. I went to bed wishing I had a mate beside me.

The next morning dawned still, clear, and cold. I piled Wooly and Zoom into the cab of the truck and drove uphill to the café. The town sparkled as if a compulsive street cleaner had swept the place spotless overnight. Not a cigarette butt was to be seen. Waxed paper, beer cans, and the careless detritus of mountain living had been swept down the canyon and deposited in a great, cosmic dustbin in the forest. Without the windows installed, the wind had blown straight through Hazel's building, sweeping the place clean of sawdust, wood scraps, and tarpaper.

I sat down in the café, ordered pancakes from Ed and began swilling coffee to warm up. The dogs followed me in, sniffed the chair legs and headed for greener pastures outdoors.

Unlike most townsfolk, Ed had a television and kept in touch with the world through the nightly news. He never spoke of body counts or massacres or moon walks, or the world situation. Instead, Ed focused on the near-at-hand, the comprehensible — a truck pile-up on the Interstate, the rescue of a high-country hiker, a cabin fire in nearby Holland. He refused to acknowledge the rest of the planet. "Can't handle it anymore," he would explain. Today, his report was about the wind. "Blew so hard last night, didn't touch down on the prairie until it found a dozen or so double-wides in a trailer park twenty miles out in the flatlands. Blew 'em apart."

Footsteps shuffled up the front steps. A thin line of men, women, and children, trooped inside and stood stiffly at attention, too cold to bend anything. The little ones moved somberly to the big coal stove that was roaring in the middle of the room. They gathered around it, consulting its warmth like a pack of tiny aliens.

"You people look like you could use something hot to eat," Ed said and headed for the kitchen.

Nobody from the rag-tag refugee band said a thing. I recognized Georgia amidst the bundles. She looked numb.

"Wind make it a tough night?" I asked.

"Blew down our teepee," Georgia said.

"What did you do for shelter?" I asked.

Georgia stared at the stove. "We gathered up the canvas, put rocks on it where the wind was coming from, and crawled underneath," she said. "We knew it had to stop sometime."

New people in the mountains are often stoic. They have no ruler to gauge what was everyday experience and what was unbearable. No, I hadn't yet survived a Montgomery winter, but the notion of huddling under a cone of violently rattling canvas seemed pretty damned stoic to me.

Oriskany Bill dashed into the café and placed a protective arm around Georgia. He whispered in her ear. The way they stood together told me that I had missed something.

Johnny LaPorte walked in the door. Ed's café was not a part of Johnny's morning routine. He walked behind the counter, poured a cup of coffee and stood there sipping as two or three more frozen communards gathered around the café stove. I wondered if things had changed for him, after our run-in with the sheriff's department.

"So," he began. "I hear you folks got blown out of your quarters last night."

The teepee folks looked at each other uncertainly.

"Pretty nasty wind out there wasn't it?" Johnny continued.

"It blew down our tent. We was cold," uttered a bundled-up, androgynous youngster.

"I bet you were, little one." Johnny turned and hollered into the kitchen. "Hey Ed, Cheryl? How 'bout if I pour coffee here? And how about some cocoa for the kids? It's on me."

Without waiting for an answer, Johnny ambled behind the counter and began setting up mugs without asking who wanted what. He just counted heads, lined up the mugs, and poured.

A young woman with bright red cheeks rode herd on the youngsters. She pulled off their mittens and showed them how to warm their hands by the stove. I recognized her as Destiny, the waif who had first arrived with the Teepee People, bloody and torn.

"You remember her?" I asked Cheryl.

"Who, Destiny? Little Miss Bad Luck? Sure," Cheryl said.

"Georgia must have prevailed," I said.

"Weather's just gonna get worse from here on in." Johnny was matter-of-fact. There was no alarm or pretense in his voice. "You're not going to want to try to winter here in that teepee."

"The original Americans did it." Michel's French accent emphasized his petulance.

"Not up here they didn't. Wasn't a red man anywhere above 5,000 feet after the snow begun to fall. They wintered down the canyons, where the livin' was easy . . .in comparison."

Johnny freshened up his coffee, came around the counter and sat down by the stove.

"So . . ." he asked. "Who's in charge here?"

"We all are," Michel proclaimed.

"Well, then," said Johnny. "Who's the oldest?"

"I can talk to you, Sheriff," said Georgia.

"Okie-doke." Johnny raised his eyes to the out of doors. "Sun's up over the ridge top now. Wind stopped. Should be gettin' pretty comfortable outside. Why don't the rest of you go sit in the sunshine, thaw out. I think Ed's fixin' some breakfast you can put in your bellies. Right, Ed?"

Ed took the cue and returned with two crates of eggs.

The frozen communards stumbled out into the sun, leaving Johnny, Michel and Georgia, Oriskany Bill, and me. Johnny smiled at the Navy castaway and nodded at the door. Oriskany Bill moved out on the porch and joined the kids, who had begun thawing out in the sunlight.

"So, what are you folks planning to do?" Johnny asked.

Georgia and Michel looked at each other. Georgia was the first to speak. "We want to stay here."

"Look," Johnny snapped. "You got a taste of what's to come. You can't camp out at 9,000 feet. It's going to get worse. Much worse. And it won't let up until April. Late April. Or May. That's seven months of wind and snow."

Michel spoke up. "There's a second wind blowing out there, Sheriff. And it's colder than the weather."

Johnny looked at Michel, his mouth pulled up at the corners in a little smile.

"This ragged group may look stupid and funny to you," Michel continued. "But we are all we have. And we have chosen to stick together."

"First of all, I'm not a sheriff. I'm the town marshal, elected and sworn in by the people of Montgomery, Colorado. If it's all the same to you, I'd rather not be confused with those people that calls themselves the Sheriff's Department. Second of all, I am here to protect and serve the people of Montgomery," he said. "All of them."

"Sorry, marshal." Georgia moved from one foot to another out of uneasiness or cold. "We didn't mean to . . ."

"Just tryin' to keep things straight. This is my bailiwick. And that means I get to worry about you."

"We can take care of ourselves," she replied. "You can't blame us for what happened to my boyfriend. I didn't even know he was here."

"Look, Georgia. I don't have anything against you," he said. "We been through a lot already and you did all right. I'm guessing you want to take care of yourselves. We all want to live free. Even me, with my short hair and my forty-hour week. I live up here because I can be my own man, just like you want to be your own woman."

"Thanks."

"You're entirely welcome, I'm sure. But you don't know how to survive at 9,000 feet. And that's where you're at. Nine thousand feet into the cold mountain air and you won't make it through the winter in that Indian teepee. You might just have time to winterize one of these abandoned cabins around here, but I can't think of how you'd all fit in, no matter how friendly you are. Which is none of my business and I don't want it to be. Besides, no matter how run-down this town looks, somebody somewhere owns every square inch of it."

Georgia's eyes narrowed. "Are you telling us we have to leave?"

"I'm saying if you all freeze to death, or if you have to be hospitalized at county expense . . ."

"That won't happen," Michel insisted.

"Hear me out," Johnny said. "First, I will feel bad for you all. It hurts to be cold. But second, you get injured or sick, you get to be my business, right then and there."

Georgia stood her ground. "We'll learn as we go."

Johnny finished his umpteenth cup of coffee. "I got to get down to Boulder before my boss figures I've quit on him. I hope I got the idea across to you. Last night was just the beginning. It's gonna get serious up here any day now. And you're not equipped for it." He put a twenty-dollar bill on the counter. "That's for the rations, Ed."

"We're going to stay," a little voice said. "We'll find a way. You wait and see. We can do anything!"

Heads turned. It was Destiny, the waif. She was standing in the doorway, away from the kids now, feet spread, arms crossed. She looked like a tiny Paul Bunyan.

Johnny looked at her for a moment, sighed, and raised his hands in supplication. He headed out the door, gave one of the teepee kids a tussle on the head and climbed aboard the Bronco. He drove off down the canyon, the radio antenna whipping in the cold clear air.

Oriskany Bill walked back into the café. "He's got a lot of nerve, telling people how to live."

"Oh, shut up, Bill," Georgia said.

Chicago Hot Blast

We set the last window into Hazel's rebuilt edifice on September twenty-second, the day that the first snow arrived in Montgomery. I say "arrived" because the flakes weren't exactly dropping out of the sky. They were seeded in the storm clouds that gathered on the other side of the Divide, and blown sideways into the town, moving ninety miles an hour from a hundred miles away. In Montgomery, the sky glared bright blue and the sun turned the snow to flying crystals. You could see the clouds from the highway, hanging behind the peaks like humongous spacecraft.

In Sullivan's absence, Eddie Warren signed on to help out. Reisinger, Eddie, and I worked inside, finishing the rough carpentry as the snow swirled through the blue sky. Now that we had the building closed in, a kerosene heater kept us warm while we boxed in the second-hand windows I found in a Boulder wrecking yard. We had shingled the roof.

We had built a stairway into the basement and we had commandeered a massive cast iron stove from the Odd Fellows' Hall across the road.

The stove could have fed a boiler on the Titanic. It was six feet tall, boasted a thick, black barrel for a body and sprouted ornate iron castings on every leg and corner. The name "Chicago Hot Blast" was cast in chrome relief above the fire door.

Installing the Chicago Hot Blast put the finishing touch on the building. We heaved the behemoth into place beneath the hole that would take the stovepipe through the first floor and up through the roof. With the last joint sealed, we stood back to admire our handiwork.

Footsteps creaked over the resawn floorboards upstairs. Boots appeared on the stairway, followed by the obligatory blue jeans, a plaid shirt, and a brand new, U.S. Air Force parka. Sullivan, looking tanned and healthy, jumped to the basement floor. "*Hasta luego, cucaracha,*" he shouted in phony Spanish. "*Qué tal, compañeros?*"

I stared at Sullivan for a full five seconds before I realized my adrenaline was rising. I had never made any progress with my inquiries among the townsfolk, none of whom knew about, or appreciated being asked, about Sullivan and the money's disappearance.

"Welcome back," I said. "You spend all of Hazel's money?"

Sullivan straight-armed me square on the chest, knocking me backwards. "I didn't take anybody's money, man," he shouted, red-faced.

Eddie stepped in, grabbed him by one arm and circled him away from me.

"It did look a little unusual," Reisinger said, "you leavin' right after that money disappeared."

"I don't know about no disappearin' money," he said, his eyes small with suspicion. "You callin' me a thief?"

"I don't care what name you go under," I said. "I want to know if you took Hazel's money."

"You do, huh?" Sullivan shook Eddie off his arm. "I'll show ya. I'll show ya's all how I make my money, motherfuckers." Sullivan started up the stairs like a stallion. "Call me a damn thief." He took the rest of the stairs three at a time.

Eddie, Reisinger, and I followed.

Sullivan stood in the newly-rebuilt room upstairs, his back to the front door. Even his parka was puffed up, he was so mad. "You ever been to Michoacan?" he said. "You know what they grow down there?"

"Yeah," said Reisinger. "Agavé plants. For tequila."

"Shit." Sullivan spit on the floor, spun on his boot heel, and marched out the door.

"Uh-oh," said Eddie, shuffling his feet and staring at the roof beams. "I think I know what's comin' next and it ain't a bottle of tequila."

Sullivan crawled into his battered aluminum camper and, within seconds, a duffle bag flew out of the pickup and landed on the road. Sullivan leapt out, dragged the bag back up the gangplank and threw it in the middle of the floor. "You think I don't pay my own way? You think I'd steal money from an old lady?"

"That's what you wanted to do a month ago," I reminded him.

Sullivan turned the duffle upside down. An avalanche of cellophane-wrapped bricks tumbled out. The cellophane gleamed dull red, yellow, and blue, stretched around the slabs of compressed marijuana.

"Shit," said Reisinger, glancing nervously out the front window.

"Pack that stuff away, fool," Eddie said and closed the door.

"Sheriff's department is all over us. They find this . . ." Reisinger picked up a brick of marijuana and smelled it. "You drag this all the way back from Mexico?"

"Yeah."

"Across the border?" Reisinger laughed, incredulous.

"No, genius. I dug a tunnel."

"Sweet Jesus," Eddie said. "You're lucky you didn't get busted thirty times over in that heap you're drivin'."

Eddie was right. Sullivan looked like a cartoon of a hippie dope dealer — scraggly beard, busted-out jeans, tie-dyed thermal undershirt. His truck was a scabrous wreck covered with bumper stickers that advised their readers to question authority, fuck the army, and do it in the road. Pig bait.

"I'm here, ain't I?" Sullivan said. "Primo, sugar-cured, Michoacan, two-point-two pounds to the brick. You do the arithmetic. That oughta pay the rent for a while. Still think I'm a thief?"

I stepped forward to offer Sullivan my hand. "Let's forget about it."

Sullivan slapped away my hand and scooped the bricks back into the bag.

Reisinger stepped between Sullivan and me. "The money's still missin'," he said. "You took off. What would you think?"

"Just to show you the kinda guy I am . . ." Sullivan tossed a brick onto the middle of the floor. "Here's one for the people," he said and exited out the door, duffle bag on his shoulder. "I'm headed for Boulder and all them dope-starved college kids.

"Careful with that shit, Sullivan," Eddie said. "You could get hurt."

Sullivan flipped us the bird, slung his cargo into the back of his pickup and motored off.

"I say we forget all about missin' money." Eddie picked up the Sullivan's brick and handed it to me. "This asshole, dead guys in the forest or the Boulder County Sheriff's department. We just moved in the Chicago Hot Blast, we

161

got a brick of Michoacan, and tomorrow's Guy Fawkes' Day. I'd call that a three-way excuse to throw a party."

In 1605, a group of Catholic gentlemen hired a soldier of fortune named Guy Fawkes to kill King James the First and the entire British Parliament. The gentlemen rented a cellar directly beneath the House of Lords and hired Fawkes to pack the space with gunpowder. Fawkes got paid a pretty penny to pack the powder and drink in the cellar until the various Lords, Commoners, and the King had assembled to open Parliament. When everyone was in place, Fawkes was to set a fuse to the gunpowder, beat a hasty retreat, and catch a fishing boat for Flanders.

Unfortunately, one of Fawkes' classy collaborators got cold feet and squawked. Fawkes was discovered biding his time in the cellar with a jug of fiery cider, a burning candle, an unlit fuse, and 36 barrels of gunpowder. The local constabulary grabbed him and slapped him on the rack where he confessed to his own guilt and coughed up the names of his employers. He and his co-conspirators were hanged two months later.

Ever since, the British people, in a baffling show of loyalty to the King James, have celebrated the exposure of the Gunpowder Plot on November fifth by burning poor Guy Fawkes in effigy. Nobody in Montgomery, Colorado, thought it was significant that we would celebrate the opening of Hazel's new building on Guy Fawkes' Day, but then, none could predict what would happen that night.

We put the word out at the café and that evening, Ed contributed a washtub full of Budweisers from the Peak to Peak café. Eddie Warren set up a vinyl-covered record player and produced a stack of scarred LPs. "Don't need no ice," Buster explained as he and Cheryl humped the beer tub up the gangplank. "Just put it on the front porch. It'll stay cool," he added. Within minutes, Montgomery's mountain crew began to rock it up to the music of Muddy Waters, Howlin' Wolf, and the Rolling Stones.

Hazel showed up early and stood near the roaring warmth of the stove pipe that radiated up from the Chicago Hot Blast, perched in the community center basement. She seemed oblivious to the pungent smell of Michoacan that rose into the air.

I took Hazel on a tour of her building. Downstairs, I pointed out the use-value of the concrete slab. "People can come in out of the cold. Work on their vehicles," I explained.

"Quite the thinker you are, Gus." Hazel smiled. "We all live on a shoestring up here, don't we? A community center will certainly come in handy." She turned and looked at me with her bright eyes. "And you seem to have gotten swept up in the spirit of things. Despite yourself."

"Despite myself?" I asked.

"When you first arrived, it seemed as if you were intent on leading the life of a metaphysician," she said, her head shaking slightly. "You had all the trappings of a hermit."

A twinge of claustrophobia shot through me, mixed with impressions from my immediate past — Katie, shotguns and teargas, the kids.

"Oh, I can read the signs," Hazel said. "Didn't I see Thoreau's Walden among your personal belongings? The mark of a man seeking solitude."

I looked at the sturdy floor above, bouncing up and down under the footsteps of revelers, doing the dirty to Otis Redding.

"Now look what you've done," she said. "Gotten yourself all caught up in the workings of our town." She began to climb the stairs towards the turmoil of shuffling, stomping feet above. "Next thing you know, you'll be running for mayor."

Juicy Brucie stuck his head down the stairway. "Mind if I look around?" he asked.

"Help yourself," I said. I opened the door of the Chicago Hot Blast and threw in another lump of coal. The heat boiled off the behemoth as if it was the sun.

"You'll want to put a railing up before long," Hazel advised me as she passed Brucie on the stairs. She nodded politely but didn't say a word. "And a collar on that stovepipe," she added. "Where it goes through the floor.

They don't call it a Chicago Hot Blast for nothing." Hazel continued her slow climb.

"Whoee," Brucie exclaimed as he landed on the new concrete slab. "Look at all the space down here. What's the old lady gonna to do? Set up an acid lab?" Brucie laughed at his own joke, then checked out the towering cast-iron hulk of the Chicago Hot Blast. "Whew," he said. "The old lady's right." He backed away from the stove.

Upstairs, Hazel stayed on. She stood by the door, bundled up in a coal-stained parka and sensible woolen trousers. Swaying slightly to the music, speaking when spoken to, she presided over us all, like a missionary visiting a tribe of heathens, blessing us with the faint trace of a smile floating serenely across her face.

By nine-thirty, we had bestowed the building with ample libations of beer and marijuana. Sullivan showed up and took credit for the pot. He got fall-down drunk and soaked up stoned compliments from stoned neighbors. All trace of anger disappeared. Still, he refused to make eye contact with me and I wasn't convinced he hadn't taken the money. But it was too late to prove anything, the building was completed, and I tried to let the past float downstream.

After Hazel left, the party settled into a second round of drinking and dancing. I stepped out of the smoke and clamor and squatted against the new building to look up at the stars. Norman and Buster joined me, cradling Budweisers between their knees.

"You know that guy you were talkin' about?" Buster settled down against the wall next to me. "That one-lunged miner?" Buster sucked on his beer. "I wanna tell y'all a little story 'bout him." He rested the beer on his knee. "He hired me one fall, gives me forty bucks and tells me to go check on his Air Stream from time to time while he's away. So I take the money and buy snow tires for the Ford. Me and Cheryl had a big Ford one-fifty then."

"Piece of crap," Norman said and joined us.

"So, this guy Carl gave you the money."

"After the first snow, I go up there, see how the old guy's trailer weathered the storm. I try the key but the lock is full of ice, so I go back to the house, boil up a kettle of water, thaw out the keyhole, open the door and VA-WOOOM . . ." Buster clamped his beer between his knees and slapped the side of the building with both hands. "This anvil goes past my ear, headed in a rapidly acceleratin' trajectory right through the trailer floor and into the snow below."

"Holy shit," I said. "What was that all about?"

"The old bastard booby trapped the Airstream! With a damn anvil! Musta figured that he'd nail anybody who tried to bust in. Never bothered to tell me. I figured he forgot."

"Downright unneighborly," Norman muttered.

"So I write Carl a nasty letter," Buster says. "I cuss him out a few times and I don't hear back from him. Few weeks later, I get this letter from his sister over in Arizona. She tells me not to bother cussin' Carl out anymore cause they found his Buick Dynaflo out in the desert one day but no Carl. Never been seen since, and they pretty much gave up on him. 'Course, bein' family, you'd think she's try to be hopeful, but she just announced it like the dog had died."

"That's the last time anybody around here has caught a glimpse or heard a word about your Carl Matthews," Norman said.

"In other words," I said, "you guys think he's dead." I contemplated my beer. "So who was I talking to in the Odd Fellows' Hall?"

"Go figure." Buster put a lip lock on the long neck of his Budweiser.

Around midnight, Eddie Warren fell off the gangplank out front. He didn't bother to get up until Norman collected him on the way home. Buster and Cheryl stood in a darkened corner and ground against each other, oblivious to the tempo changes in the music. Malfese whirled like a demented dervish until he danced a hole in the floor. His foot went through a weak point in the subfloor and he sunk up to his knee in splintered wood until we rescued him.

Georgia never showed. She and the Teepee People hadn't come back to town since they had gotten blown out of their campsite by the wind but Jewel had been on the prowl all night. She danced an orbit around me like a sexy satellite, blinking her big eyes like a cartoon seductress, humming happily to herself.

The music stopped and the party dissolved, leaving Jewel looking up at the moon through the clear, small-paned windows I had installed.

I came up behind her.

"Why do you suppose Hazel did this?" Jewel asked without turning around.

"Did what?" I said, smelling her hair.

"Paid you to build a community center for a bunch of hippies."

"Maybe she's getting into the spirit of the times," I said.

"What is the spirit of the times?"

The moon smiled down. The new-old building smelled of beer and marijuana. The left-over rhythms of John Lee Hooker and Michel Butterfield grooved in my head.

"In China, they had an epidemic of disease carried by flies," I said. "There were billions of flies everywhere, in the sewage, on the food, drinking out of babies' eyes."

"Yech."

"They decided that every day, every person in China should kill ten flies. They spread the word. Every day, each and every person killed ten flies. In two years they got rid of the flies."

"What did the flies have to say about that?"

" 'Why, just look at that,' they said 'These hippies just built their own original, up-from-the-grass-roots collective. No Chinese Long March, no Russian politboro, just presto! Our own baby revolution."

"Jeez, Gus. You rebuilt a building from nothing. And it's totally cool. Does it have to be a revolution, too?"

"Probably not." I loved Jewel for her straight-ahead view of the world. No put downs, just a cool-it regard for all things big or little. She made me feel good. "Look." I pointed to the moon. "She digs it, too."

"Who?" she asked. "The moon?"

"Yeah," I said. "And Hazel.

Jewel's hair glistened in the shadows.

"What do I know? Maybe she's going to turn it into a tourist bureau and sell rooms by the night in the Odd Fellows' Hall."

Jewel caressed my temples with her fingertips. "Buddy boy," she said. "You think too much." She stroked the back of my neck and kissed me full on the lips.

"Mmm," I said. "Sun warmed."

"Sun warmed?" she asked.

"Your lips. Like blackberries when you pick 'em and eat 'em."

"So, at least you got good taste. That's a start."

"And you taste good." I grinned.

"I assume that was a compliment," she said.

"Uh huh."

"Flattery will get you everywhere," she said. "Let's clean up."

We threw beer bottles and paper plates stained with spaghetti into the big trash can. Ginger with drunkenness, we climbed down the steep stairs to the basement. We banked the fire in the Chicago Hot Blast, scattering the embers in the firebox, making sure nothing glowed behind the thick layer of quartz riveted into its ancient door.

All was quiet. The stove pipe ticked as it cooled. After I pulled the door closed, Jewel took me by her mittened hand and led me down the springy gangplank to the lonesome road.

I shivered.

"You cold?" she asked.

"Goose must have stepped on my grave."

"Boy, what a time for bleak thoughts."

Together we stumbled down the hill to her cabin. Inside, the close warmth of the kitchen fire carried her smell. Jewel made tea and I sat at her table.

"Look at you," she said as she filled a Chinese teapot full of lapsang soochong. "Nobody has been able to talk that old lady into the price of an ice cream sundae and here you are, sitting on a season's work, a brand new building, and visions of world domination."

"World revolution," I said.

She handed me a mug of hot tea. "Who was it, cute guy with a beret and a gun, he said a revolutionary gets guided by great feelings of love."

"Che Guevara."

"So, when you gonna try the 'great feelings of love' part?"

"Whattya mean?"

Jewel straddled my blue-jeaned legs, put her sweet-smelling arms around my neck, and kissed me slowly on the lips.

Blindly, I put my tea mug on the table.

In her bed she climbed atop me once again, sweet, white thighs arching over the tangle where we came together. We moved slowly against each other in the warm light of the kerosene lantern while her dog snoozed and sighed on the carpet, out of sight at the foot of the bed.

DREAMS

A grenade exploded, shattering glass in a wall of windows. Shrapnel splattered against wood. Glass shards of tear gas permeated a bedroom. A baby shrieked over the percussive flutter of an owl's wings. A woman shouted my name but I couldn't see. I was tangled in a nest of electrical wire and I shouted soundlessly.

I woke up.

"Gus!" The night air was cold and still. Jewel stood at the window in her nightgown. "Get up!" Tongues of red and orange light flickered on the bedroom wall. Her dog barked at the kitchen door. The sound was explosive. I got out of bed, cold air shrinking my skin. "Something's burning," she said. "Look." She made room for me at the window.

The sky was lit with cinders; they glowed as they slid up a tower of angry smoke. A pickup truck whined past.

"That's the center of town," I said, stumbling into my trousers. "My socks," I cursed, my hands shaking. "Where are my socks!" I scuffled into the street, boots unlaced, Jewel's dog racing up the road ahead of me.

Eddie Warren pulled up in his truck and I jumped on the running board, my hands freezing in the wind. We roared up Left Hand Canyon Road and rounded the bend. Flame belched out of every window in Hazel's brand-new, recycled storefront. Flowers of fire blossomed around the chimney and flew into the sky, reflected from every cabin window on the hillside.

Uphill, headlights gathered at the old barn where the fire engines were kept. Eddie stopped in front of the burning building and I jumped off.

"Stay here," he hollered. "I got the key to the fire shed."

I stared at the flames.

"Don't move," Eddie shouted through the passenger window. "You hear me? Don't do anything stupid. We'll be right back." Eddie powered up the road against the roar of the flames.

Shock ran through my body like electricity but there was nothing I could do. Mute, out of breath, I stood frozen to the ground, protecting my face with a forearm. The heat and angry motion of combustion pushed me back. I watched the rafters ignite while my face tightened with the heat and my ass froze in the cold night air.

The town truck pulled onto the scene, loaded with local firefighters. Reisinger jumped out from behind the wheel, grim and self-important in his long-johns and cowboy hat.

I glared at him. What kind of a fool wears a cowboy hat to a fire? My building was burning down. I must be doing it wrong. I turned superstitious. I had transgressed against my real life, back in the city — the theater collective, Katie, the kids. This conflagration was the payback. I caught myself and began to haul the canvas hose out of the truck.

Johnny showed up, furious, a parka covering his undershirt. "You see what we got here?" he shouted toothlessly in my face. "We got people running around with their dicks in their hands. Jesus Christ."

There was no adapter for the hydrant. Amidst shouts and countermands, the volunteers scrambled to find the missing link while the front of Hazel's community center ate itself for breakfast.

Norman pulled the adapter out from under the passenger's seat of the truck. With the hoses hooked up we had water on the fire in minutes. The flames retreated, but not before Hazel's structure had burnt to a cross-hatch tangle of wet, stinking, carbonized sticks.

I sat on the ground and stared at the smoking ruin. Sad, serious faces peered through windows, crowbars and axes broke out hot spots, and gloved hands dragged frozen, charcoal-covered hoses through the slush.

Jewel came up behind me and clasped her arms across my chest.

I pulled her hand to my cheek. "I don't understand," I said.

"Understand what?"

"What I did wrong."

"You didn't do anything wrong, you lunatic. It's bigger than that."

"What's that supposed to mean?"

"I mean, fire is elemental. And part of the planet."

"Drop the hippie crap," I snapped. "Nothing mystical about a fire."

Jewel pulled her hand away. "Who said there was?"

"I wasn't that drunk," I said. "We checked the stove."

"You're just pissed off. Who wouldn't be? It wasn't your fault."

"This isn't about fault." I could feel the anger rising, hard. "Shit." Again, I smothered it. "Something went down here. Some kinda weird shit."

"You may be right." She gave my shoulder a squeeze. "If something weird. . ."

"Or somebody."

"Okay, if somebody did fuck this place up, it'll come out. You know that. This is the mountains. In the meantime . . ." She pulled me to my feet. "We got a pile of crap to clean up." She crossed the road to help the others.

Down the canyon, the red and blue lights of a police car flickered against the tin-rust front of the Odd Fellows' Hall. A sheriff's Blazer pulled up and stopped. The leather-jacketed driver leaned out the window. Officer Rowdy again. Didn't this guy ever sleep? "What is this mess?" he asked Johnny.

Johnny refused to answer. He didn't have his teeth in; he wasn't going to make a fool of himself for the benefit of any Boulder County Sheriff.

I got up and walked over to the Blazer. "Had a little fire here, officer," I said warmly. I felt calm, almost magnanimous.

"Sure did."

"We got it under control."

"You people. You're gonna to have to report this, y'know. Structure fire." He looked up at the smoking frame. "This the same place just got built?"

I nodded. "Yep." I was amazed at my own bright tone. "Hazel Gunther's property."

"She know about it?" He lit a Marlboro.

Perfect, I thought. *Sheriff Rowdy, the Marlboro Man.*

"Not yet," I replied. "I'll tell her in the morning."

"Yeah. Let the old broad get her beauty rest." He motioned towards Johnny, who was furiously coiling hose. "What's wrong with El Jefe over there? Cat got his tongue?"

"He's just trying to get things wrapped up. Got to get to work in the mornin', ya know."

He looked at me and raised one eyebrow. "On a Sunday?" Rowdy put the big black Blazer in gear, then stopped. "By the way . . ."

I turned.

"We checked out that stiff you people found up in the forest. Turns out he was part of some group back in California. The Weather Man or Underground Man. I dunno. Some new type of your left-wing militants. We figure with him dead, that'll wrap up the dynamite problem. Gone but not forgotten." He winked and gave me a phony salute. "Stay tuned. You'll be hearin' from us." The Blazer took off toward the café.

We loaded the sodden, soot-filled hose back onto the truck.

I sat by the road until a dishwater dawn illuminated the scene. Tendrils of smoke and steam were the only things moving in the scorched community center. I wasn't ready to face Hazel yet. I trudged downhill to my place. Wooly and Zoom sniffed at my trousers and looked up at me, curious.

"Yeah. That's fire you smell." I filled their pans. "Dad's night out. Eve of destruction."

I put on water for coffee and watched the dogs. Their pans were full, they would scarf down breakfast, take a shit, eat more, and go back to sleep. For them, a new day was dawning, just like any other day, a day full of food, fleas, dog naps, and a romp in the woods. They didn't have any problems. They were the dogs.

Despite Jewel's gentle cajolery, I had plenty to think about. For one thing, if I hadn't been shot in the ass back in Berkeley on Bloody Thursday, I probably wouldn't be standing here in front of the burnt-out hulk of a summer's work. And I probably would have joined the Weather Underground alongside Georgia's shotgun-blasted boyfriend.

By Bloody Thursday, the Weather Underground had already begun its split with the antiwar movement. They were pushing for big change and they were pushing fast. As antiwar protestors, they had tried everything — non-violence, peaceful protest, petitioning, silent demonstrations. Nothing had slowed the juggernaut. Now they were all desperate and angry as I had been while Katie pulled Blue Meanie buckshot out of my ass — no place to run, no place to hide. Up against the wall, they resolved to tear the roof off the motherfucker. Anger. Fury. Days of rage. Burn it, blow it up, whatever it took to destroy the corporate death machine.

The Weather Underground wanted to get crazy, but they knew who the enemy was — and wasn't. Their battle would not be fought against everyday people. No. The people were their allies, to be won over. Instead, they would bomb state property — FBI offices, defense research labs, draft boards — detonating their explosives late at night when nobody was around. Property, not people. That was their thing.

So what was Georgia's boyfriend doing, smuggling dynamite to blow up power poles. Sure, power poles fed navy port facilities but they also wired hospitals, schools, working people's homes. It didn't make sense. Not even for the Weather Underground. They were pissed and unpredictable but they weren't sloppy. So why?

Fuck, my head hurt.

I sat down on the cabin floor with the *I Ching* and I threw down the coins onto the rough wood.

"The Corners of the Mouth," it read. I turned to the dogs "Either one of you guys understand this reading?"

Wooly pushed his pie tin under the stove. Zoom licked his balls.

The *I Ching* was a rag. A three-thousand-year-old bingo game invented by charlatans. Some fool in Berkeley became obsessed with the logarithmic probabilities of the I Ching's sixty-four hexagrams and calculated that both the *I Ching* and the Mayan calendar ended at 2012. A double apocalypse. Damn! That was too far ahead to imagine. I was pretty sure we'd all be dead by then. Besides, the book was bullshit. "The corners of the mouth," I grumbled. "The corners of my ass."

LETTERS OF FIRE AND SWORD

Hungry dogs brought me back to a cold Colorado morning, a dead body in the King's Forest and a charred building in Montgomery. Today I had to tell Hazel. She invited me in and sat me down on her verandah while she put the kettle on. I sat in her easy chair, waiting for the pot to boil, eyes blurred by fatigue. She set a pot of tea on the table in front of us and placed knobby-knuckled hands on her knees.

"Well, Gus, how may I help you?"

"Hazel," I blurted out. "Your building burned down last night."

"Oh, my." She clasped her hands in her lap and sat quietly, head shaking gently with her palsy.

A clock ticked from inside the house.

"I shut the stove down myself. I was the last to leave."

She put a hand on my arm. "Whenever I'm confused by circumstances, I turn to the dictionary."

"Huh?"

"The dictionary. It contains so much, you know." She disappeared into her sitting room.

The dictionary. A smile tugged at the corners of my mouth. The corners of my mouth? Goddamned I Ching. I followed.

She flicked through the pages of a massive Oxford dictionary on a stand. "Hmmmm. Let me see. Fire, fire . . ." She licked her fingers and snapped another page.

A clock ticked ponderously in the hall.

"Here it is." Hazel leaned closer. " *'Fire.'* From the German. Oh yes, *'The natural agency or active principal involved in combustion.'* Well, that's clear, isn't it?" Her gnarled finger held her place. " *'With reference to hell or purgatory,'* " she continued. " *'To inflame, excite intensely. To make a brilliant reputation.'* Well," she said, "I certainly hope that was not your motivation, Gus. To improve your reputation." She gave an adolescent snicker. Her building had burnt and she didn't seem to give a damn.

"Oh, here's an interesting tidbit," she said vacantly. " *'Letters of fire and sword — an order authorizing a sheriff to dispossess an obstinate tenant or proceed against a delinquent by any means in his power.'* " Hazel turned to me, eyebrows raised. "But then, we mustn't take these definitions too literally, should we?" She dove back into the big book. She contemplated burning heat produced by disease, a burning passion or feeling, dismissed the "*action of firing guns*," and with an "A-ha!" landed on " '*to encounter or face the greatest dangers or to submit to the severest ordeal or proof.* ' "

She shut the dictionary, closed her eyes and sat back into an old easy chair. "So there it is," she said. "Your fire was a test. Mister Bessemer, a test of our courage, of our persistence. And don't you notice? The word 'fire' bears a striking resemblance to the word 'fear.' Did you notice that?"

I stood before her, speechless. Out of the Oxford English Dictionary Hazel had created a workable definition of this indecipherable disaster. And it seemed to satisfy her. I scrambled to recall the words: to submit to proof, fire and fear, and — most vividly — "an order authorizing a sheriff to dispossess an obstinate tenant." *Letters of fire and sword.*

Hazel saw me to the door. "You know, Gus," she said. "We can learn from every incident in our lives." She opened her door onto the gray winter day and gently ejected me out of her house and her consciousness. I hadn't yet finished my tea.

Slate-gray clouds hung over the town. The wind had begun to blow. I wrapped the hood of my parka around my chin and plodded uphill toward Hazel's building. The front of the community center stared at me like an abused child. Tears of ash stained the siding beneath each window. The gangplank lay tumbled in the ditch by the road and burnt bits of roofing filled the alley. On the roof, a half-torn sheet of tin clattered in the wind.

I clambered onto the front porch. The door had been chopped through. Inside, a ragged hole gaped where the stovepipe had come through the floor. A burnt circle in the roof framed the gray sky like an open lens. I walked to the charred hole in the floor and peered down.

I was staring into the epicenter of a detonation. The Chicago Hot Blast stood unscathed in the gloom beneath a jumble of burnt flooring. Before it had twisted and collapsed in the heat, the stove pipe had ignited both floor and ceiling. In the middle of the night, the cast iron behemoth had become a firebomb. But Jewel and I had banked that fire before we left, leaving nothing but a heap of ash at the bottom of the grate. I was sure. Or had I been too drunk? Had I forgotten something?

I tiptoed down the blackened stairs ready to jump if they collapsed, pushing my way through the carbonized mess, prying planks and two-bys out of the way until I could peer into the mica eye of the Hot Blast. I pulled off my gloves, lifted the heavy latch, and opened the firebox door.

Inside, a tight mound of coals lay water-soaked and compacted beneath the grill. I thrust in my hand and sifted through the mush. There, at the bottom, my fingers found metal. I brought out two, three nails, congealed glass, and the remains of a tin can. I had started the fire in the Hot

Blast before the party began. As a first-time ritual, I had carefully and lovingly stacked clean, straight-cut pieces of kindling on the cast-iron grid. The ash box had been brushed and empty — no debris — when I began my little ceremony.

Someone else had visited the Chicago Hot Blast after we staggered down the hill to Jewel's cabin. I pictured a figure crouching in the cold, quiet darkness, soaking splinters of scrap wood and coal with kerosene while I lay on my back a couple of hundred yards away, enveloped in bliss. I stood up, looked around at the fire-blackened chaos and decided to get out of there — fast.

Who would destroy a community center? And why? Sure, I had accused Sullivan of stealing money. But was that a motive for arson? The punishment didn't fit the crime. Besides, he left the party so piss-drunk, I doubt that he could have lit his own ass on fire, much less torch a building. When in doubt . . .

I headed for the café.

Cheryl and Buster were sitting in a corner, eating breakfast with Norman. Sullivan was sitting at the counter, talking to Ed. Juicy Brucie turned and looked at me. I couldn't read his watery gray eyes. Was he laughing at me? One by one, the others turned toward me, their faces open, expectant. I stood at the door, staring at the people of Montgomery like they were characters in a Norman

Rockwell painting. Did one of these people burn Hazel's building? Did one of them kill a man in the King's Forest?

I took the whole scene in, turned around and walked out the door. I felt alone, crazy, desperate, like a dope fiend in Sunday school, like a communist in suburbia, like a demon in heaven. What was I doing in this god-forsaken place with winter coming on like gangbusters?

I stepped into the café phone booth and called Katie.

She let me talk.

"My building burnt down last night," I blurted.

"Huh?"

"My building. The community center."

"Gus, what are you talking about?" She sounded strange, a stranger. "What building?"

"Mine."

"You own a building?"

"The community center. The one I just built. It burned down. I think somebody torched it. I can't figure out why." I could hear the kids clamoring in the background, distant, distant, so far away. "Look, a lot's been going on here, not all of it good. The town marshal thinks . . ."

" 'The town marshal'? You got a marshal?"

"He lives up here. He's a lawman, but he's one of us. Sort of. He's got this theory that the Man is trying to clear hippies out of mountains."

"Boy, Gus, you sure know how to find the action."

"And a guy got killed up here."

"What?"

"A guy got killed."

"Shit. Who?" Katie asked. "Somebody from the town?"

"Word has it, he's a Weather Underground guy. They think he was here smuggling dynamite." I looked out over the town. The colors were muted by the lead-gray sky.

"Oh, wow," she whispered. "Somebody in Colorado is sending dynamite out here," Katie said. Her voice sounded strained and low. "Least that's what the papers say. They say the bombers used dynamite from Colorado. They just blew up a bunch of high-tension power lines in Port Chicago. It's the second time in a couple of weeks. The papers out here are squawking about left-wing militants and sabotage and all that."

"But it can't be him," I shouted.

"Who? What can't be him? Dammit, Gus, make some sense here."

"The cops here, the Sheriff's department, they say they found the dynamite smuggler. They think it was the dead guy we found in the national forest."

"Stop! Stop! My phone." She blew her breath into the mouthpiece. "You better be careful, Gus. The world is smaller than you think."

"No kidding," I said.

"Be careful. Please. I gotta go." She turned away from the phone. "Kids, I told you . . ."

The phone clicked. Wind burbled in my ears. A dial tone cut in and I was alone, standing in a glass box in the wilderness, holding a cold earpiece on the end of a metal-covered cord.

Duck Lake

Oriskany Bill scuffed into Ed's café and sat down next to Norman and me. "We're gonna liberate Duck Lake," he said.

"You're what?" Norman said.

"Liberate. Li-ber-ate! The lodge. You know, the old resort, up at the Lake. We're gonna move in."

"Who's we?" asked Norman.

"The whole family." Bill had taken to calling Georgia and the Teepee People "the family."

"We got it all planned out," Bill continued. "Truck on up there just before the first snow falls. By the time they find out, it'll be too late. We'll be home free for the winter."

"Duck Lake in the winter. 'Home free' ain't exactly what comes to mind," Norman said.

Duck Lake was the Jewel in a necklace of alpine lakes that descended from the high country above Montgomery.

Duck Lake summers consisted of warm days and cool evenings. Because it lay above 10,000 feet, the resort was beyond the range of the devilish mountain mosquitoes that swarmed around the edges of lakes at lower altitudes. But in the winter, Hazel had explained, winds blew unceasingly without anything to slow their velocity, through the dragon's mouth of the passes, down the glaciers, across the tundra, and into the stunted forests around Duck Lake. Day after day, icy blasts of air blew at speeds of 60, 80, 100 miles per hour. It was ferocious, intolerable, and if the cold didn't freeze you, the constant buffeting would drive you insane.

"No one ever stayed a winter at Duck Lake," Norman said. "Not the foolhardiest adventurer, not the drunkenest miner, not the craziest trapper. Hell. No one's even tried." Norman stared into his coffee cup.

Oriskany Bill babbled on, undaunted, his eyes bright with the beauty of his plan. They would haul enough canned goods to last them the winter. The lodge had a huge fireplace. That would be their central gathering place. They would live in style and let the wind blow. In the good weather, they'd venture out to hunt. They'd have it made in the shade.

The number of times that Bill referred to Georgia told me that the man was in love. I thought of her and all the rest of those tender young hippies, freezing to death in the howling, snow-filled wind. Even a greenhorn with my limited experience told me they were nuts. Listening to

Oriskany Bill's alarmingly stupid scheme gave me claustrophobia. I paid up and clumped out of the café.

Outside, traces of snow scudded past. Without the sun, the cold was sharp, and the wind bit at my ears. Reisinger and his pretty wife drove past me. He saluted. She gave me a tentative wave and a sympathetic little smile but they didn't stop. I was glad. They looked out of place in their battered flatbed truck. They needed a station wagon full of kids, a house where they could begin the long sleepwalk through a dream guaranteed by wars and moonwalks, kangaroo courts, and superhighways.

I let the wind blow me downhill on foot. The white smoke of a new fire whisked out of Jewel's chimney. I saw movement behind the kitchen window and smelled the fragrance of piñon smoke. The smell brought me back to the comfort of her gentle, fatalistic chiding. "A mystery is just that. Don't dig too deep and don't be so hard on yourself."

Yeah, I could have knocked on Jewel's door, but I didn't want comfort. I had a pocket full of pieces I couldn't put together, a bowl full of nails I couldn't chew, and an anger I couldn't swallow. I knew too much; I didn't know enough. I kept a cold shoulder to the wind and snow, trudged past my charred edifice, and clambered up into the gaping maw of the Odd Fellows' Hall.

I stood in the barren silence of the big, high-ceilinged space and listened to the building bend to the wind. Each gust set off a woody chorus of creaks and pops as the timbers and tin of the big structure swayed as it had for nearly a century. A sense of peace hung in the big, ungainly space, like standing in the middle of a ballroom after the party was over.

I heard a cough and the sound of a chair being dragged over the splintered boards of the second floor. An eerie calm settled into my bowels. I knew who I wanted to talk to. I climbed loudly, to give the old miner warning that I was there. When I reached the top stair he was there, jammed into his chair, facing the dirty window. The Odd Fellows' Hall shook with a gust of wind that rattled away like the diminishing roll of a thunderclap.

"Hey, Carl."

He twitched, startled, turned from the neck up, caught me in the corner of his eye, and grunted. The grunt evoked a wheeze and a paroxysm of coughing that doubled the old man over his bony knees.

"You all right?" I asked.

He glared at me and doubled over again, convulsed by a second round of coughing. When the attack left him, Carl swung his chair in a tight arc on the splintered floor. He sat facing me, coffee mug in hand, big ears sticking out from the ragged shock of his self-cut hair. His features were lost in the backlight of the window but I could see he was wearing the same clothes he had on when I met him: a dirty plaid mackinaw and stained khakis turned up at the cuffs.

He picked up a tarnished aluminum percolator and poured himself a cup of coffee. The dark liquid steamed as it flowed into the white mug. I didn't see a burner anywhere. He leaned over, took a flat pint bottle of Four Roses out of his Mackinaw jacket and poured a dollop into his cup. He sipped the steaming brew and stared at me over the rim. "Scared the hell out of me," he said and rested the coffee cup on the arm of the chair. "What you want?"

"You mind?" I asked, trudging into the gloom to retrieve a tumbled bentwood chair.

"Make any diff'rence if I did?"

I dropped my gloves on the floor and sat down.

Carl took another slurp of his coffee. "Seen your building burnt down."

"Yeah."

"On Guy Fawkes Day. That's rich." He laughed. "A penny for the Guy." The cough doubled him over again. "Told ya this place was full of trouble," he offered when he recovered. "'Course nobody listens to an old fart like me. I'm used to it by now."

Outside, the wind blew with a slow, steady shriek.

"You know," I began. "When I came out here from California, I thought I was gonna cool out, get my head together. You know, slow down, unwind, take time to think."

"Think?! What you wanna do that for?"

I ignored him. "Instead I walk into this weird, fucked up other world, no different from the one I just left. Cynics, dreamers, pissed-off citizens with no power to change anything, not enough money, too many cops. Strife, tribulation, and rage at injustice. It's here, it's back home, it's everyplace. You can't get away, no matter how hard you try. Not if you got two eyes and a brain in your head."

"And a mouth in your face."

I looked at the old man. He looked as if he didn't give a damn what he or anybody else said. That was good. I could keep rapping. "Like, for instance . . . " I paused while he swigged his coffee, now mostly whiskey. "We found a dead guy up in the forest."

Silence.

"And then, right after we bring the body down to Johnny's, two Blazer loads of Boulder County Sheriffs show up. Now figure that. Somebody must have ratted out somebody else somewhere. Right?"

He smoothed his throat with another swig. "Maybe."

"I mean, we didn't tell anyone about the dead guy."

"Who's 'we'?" he asked. "Those sad-sacks you got in town down there?"

"We all agreed. 'Let Johnny handle it,' we said."

"'We all agreed,'" he mimicked. "Somebody must have disagreed. The Boulder County boys showed up uninvited."

"Then Hazel's place goes up in flames. It doesn't make sense. Jewel and me, we checked the stove before we left."

"Jewel, huh? Sounds female. You plunkin' some little lady in town here?" He groaned. "Lucky bastard. Shit. You just wait. You wait 'til you're an old man like me. You still want some — that don't never change — but you can't get it, not for love or money. Shit." He cackled, spit again, and rubbed his crotch with his free hand. "One helluva world." He looked at me, his jug-eared head tilted.

"Thing is . . ." I leaned toward the old man. "Somebody's smuggling dynamite out of Colorado. To blow up stuff in California. Only they're blowing up the wrong stuff!"

"Now what the hell are you talkin' about?"

"Colorado dynamite going off in California."

"Who? Buncha communists?"

No, they're saying it's antiwar people. That's bullshit."

"How d'you know that?"

"Because I know them. They aren't about blowing up power poles. They're trying to work with the unions out there, the guys that load the ships."

"What ships?"

"Old Liberty ships left over from World War Two. They load ammunition on these rust buckets for Vietnam. A lot of people against the war been putting up picket lines."

"Fat lotta good that'll do." He buried his nose in his coffee mug.

"And that's where the power poles got dynamited," I said. "It doesn't make sense. I mean, those antiwar people, they're trying to get the longshore guys to stop loading the ships."

Carl rubbed his grizzled face. "Back in the '30s, '36 or so, there was a big flap like that. Longshoreman wouldn't load scrap iron for Japan. They didn't like what the Japanese were doin' at the time, which was fucking the Chinks in the ass."

"Okay. Same here. So why would the anti-war guys be blowing up power poles, the same time they're trying to work with the longshoremen? It doesn't make sense to me."

"What about that stiff?" he asked. "He's probably the one causin' all the trouble."

"That's what the sheriff's department thinks. But this dead guy, he was Weather Underground."

"Jesus H. Christ. You're so goddamn full of names it's a wonder your head don't explode. Now who you talking about. Ain't no weather underground. Nothing but rock and water."

"Weather Underground people are hardcore antiwar. They want to bomb shit, but not houses. Just FBI offices."

"Best of luck to 'em," he growled.

"Last I heard, the Weather Underground people were still tight with everybody. They wouldn't sabotage another antiwar action. At least not yet."

Carl ignored me. "Guy Fawkes got caught playin' with black powder. They put him on the rack."

"I was just talking to my girlfriend out in San Francisco."

"You got pussy stashed all over the place, don't ya?" he whined.

"My girlfriend says somebody blew up more power poles out there, just a few nights ago. So this guy we found in the forest, that was more'n a month ago. He can't have much to do with it, can he?"

"How would you know? Maybe he shipped enough nitro to blow up half of 'Frisco. But I'll tell ya one goddamned thing." He slugged back the bottom of the coffee and whiskey. "This town has a history of puttin' people through shit, and you, my young fool, are steppin' in it like a dago in a wine vat. If I was you, I'd put two and two together."

"Great. How?"

"Number one. You got dynamite, a dead body, and a burnt-out building here in Montgomery. Number two. There's people in California, they got orders to start trouble."

"Who does?" I asked.

Carl glared at me like I was stupid. "The ones doin' the dynamitin'."

He stopped to cough, hard. Doubled over.

"You all right?"

He waved me away. "You push them too hard, they'll come out of hiding to fight you. Keep it up, Beelzebub.

They'll kill you sure as they'll kill a gook in a rice paddy."
Carl continued, "You people are trying to do somethin'
bigger'n dumber'n anything I seen for a while. More power
to ya. But they's other, bigger people, don't want you to do
it. So . . ." He took another swig of his coffee. "You look to
them for yer troublemakers. It's always the big guys start the
trouble," he said. "Little guy can't afford to. Little guy wants
to go home, read the newspaper, have a coupla beers, maybe
get laid, raise a family. Nobody picks on a bully, right?"

"Yessir, I figured that out early."

"Number three: The big boys, they won't hesitate.
They'll use the letters of fire and sword if they got to, just to
make it happen."

I frowned. *Letters of fire and sword.*

"And whatever you do," Carl continued, "don't turn
your back on it. You run, you'll pay for it the rest of your
life. You push them, they push back and don't kid yourself.
They got more guns than you people got sense."

"They got the guns," I said, "and you're tellin' me not
to run. Why?"

"Ain't life a bitch?" Carl began to cough. A shattering
convulsion knocked the coffee cup out of his hand. I moved
to pick up the cup. Still coughing, he gestured me away.
"Out," he gasped. "Leave me alone."

RETREAT

Wooly and Zoom followed me back to the cabin. I started a fire in the stove and went outside to buck a spar of standing deadwood from the King's Forest. As I split wood, I tried to put other pieces together.

Hazel had quoted letters of fire and sword from the dictionary. Something about sheriffs and delinquents and dispossessed tenants, she said. Letters of fire and sword. Dead or alive, how did Carl dig up the same words?

Carl was right about one thing: You push them, they push back. You push too hard, they step out from behind the curtain and smash you. Sure, you can wear your hair long and smoke dope. Play loud music and dress funny, live on top of one another, give each other the clap, teach your own children, but if you boycott their corporations or trash their university weapons labs, if you put your shoulders to the big wheels, they'll fight back. They'll come after you, regular, methodical, like it's their job. It is their job. They got the time and they got the guns. The other part of Carl's commentary I couldn't swallow. "Don't turn your back on it," he said. "You run, you'll pay for it the rest of your life." Berkeley or Montgomery, run or no run, trouble kept lurking around in paradise and I was right in the middle of it. I was beginning to believe in karma. Don't turn your back on it. Hell, I needed to turn my back on it, I needed to run.

By the time I had bucked and split a shoulder-high pyramid of clean, white wood, I had a plan. First, I was going to stay away from people, dead or alive. Second, I was going to rebuild Hazel's storefront — by myself. Wooly and Zoom and me, we were going to get down with Henry David Thoreau. Walden Pond at 9,000 feet. Fuck the Weather Underground, the Mobe Against the War, agents provocateurs, dynamite smugglers, dead guys, and invisible snitches.

Fuck Jewel, Georgia, the Teepee People and their crazy tough-it-out winter scheme. Fuck Marshal Johnny LaPorte and IBM and the STP Gang and the Boulder County Sheriff's Department. Fuck 'em all. They could take the whole package of personal sadness, sorrow, stupidity, and pathos, take the unmitigated political and economic violence and stink of overwhelming, entrenched corporate capitalist power, put it in a garbage bag, tie it up in the coils of Katie's tapped phone wire, turn it sideways, and shove it up the collective ass of the cosmos.

The next morning, I nailed the four corners of a sign to my door that said —

OUT OF TOWN
BE BACK SOMETIME

I didn't leave. Instead, I covered the windows of Hazel's building with canvas, set up a pot belly stove I salvaged from an abandoned mine and commenced to tear out the building's burnt parts. The pile of charred lumber grew beneath the rear windows while December clouds flew overhead in stop-action. Nobody bothered me. Winter closed in and people stayed inside or moved around sluggishly like ants in a cold snap.

I ripped off a short stack of half-inch plywood from a construction site in the foothills above Boulder. I chose a big, fat developer's site, not some poor guy's twenty acres. In good weather, I got back up in the rafters and nailed down a new plywood roof from the liberated four-by-eight sheets. A one-legged hippie from Jamestown milled raw pine logs into flooring and I nailed it over the refurbished joists.

The dogs kept me company, sleeping all day next to the stove. When they weren't snoozing in the community center, Wooly and Zoom ranged around town, poking into garbage and sniffing butt holes. I bought a new set of used windows from a wrecking yard in Boulder. I copped a bentwood chair from the Odd Fellows' Hall. After the windows were in, I stopped work whenever I felt like it and sat in the bentwood chair, feeding the fire with wood scraps. The Chicago Hot Blast sat cold but intact in the basement like a sleeping giant.

Well, maybe I didn't believe in revelations, but the image of my old man came to me, standing alone as the bus drove away. I guess that was an epiphany of sorts. I cradled the image as I began to cry in the warm winter sunshine. I looked around to see if anyone was watching, then sat down before the fire and bawled like a baby. For the first time, I missed my old man.

Georgia Descends

With my old man gone, I got lonesome. Kind of ironic. He must have been keeping me company throughout this sojourn. So, on the shortest day of the year — and one of the coldest and windiest I had experienced in my mountain getaway — I trucked up to the café to check in. I didn't want to sit alone anymore certainly not in the long dark of the winter solstice.

Nothing had changed. Juicy Brucie sat at the counter watching Cheryl and Buster scarf down Ed's soup de jour.

"Look what the dog dragged in," Buster said.

I took a cup of coffee from Ed and joined them.

"That sign on your cabin door still up?" Cheryl asked.

"I needed time to think," I said.

"That's a switch," Buster said. "Most people up here work overtime to keep from thinkin'."

"Learn anything?" Ed asked.

"That I get lonesome."

"Jewel's back in town," Cheryl said.

"Where'd she go?" I asked.

Cheryl laughed. "Where you been?"

Georgia walked in the door, bundled up like a kid in a sooty orange snowsuit. Her face was ruddy with wind and coal smoke and she had big circles under her eyes. She asked Ed for a cup of tea and shuffled to a booth on the far side of the stove.

"Get yourself a meal, Georgia." Buster hollered from across the room. "It's on me."

Georgia smiled and gave us a child's wave. She still had on her mittens.

Ed brought her the cup of tea. She pulled her mittens off, put her hands around the cup, and focused on the empty seat across the table.

Brucie couldn't believe his eyes. A real live single female was sitting right there in an otherwise empty booth looking helpless and forlorn. Love, lust or predatory opportunism swelled in Brucie's breast and propelled him across the café to Georgia's booth where he hovered like an apologetic vulture. "Hi."

She looked up, blinked once, returned her attention to the opposite seat.

Brucie slid into the seat beside her. "Where's the rest of your friends?"

"Get lost," she said.

He pushed his face to inches from hers. "You look terrible."

"So do you."

"You need to thaw out. Why don't you come down to my place?"

Cheryl was about to intercede. No need. Georgia shifted her butt into the corner of Ed's knotty-pine booth, placed one booted foot on the side of Brucie's rump and pushed. He landed on the floor with a thump, his face a cartoon of surprise.

Buster let out an open-mouth guffaw that launched a mouthful of pancake across the counter.

Georgia headed for the bathroom.

Brucie glared up us with his gray wolfen eyes. "Shut up, you bastards." He pulled himself to his feet and stomped out.

Georgia returned, got her tea, and sat down at the counter. "Those assholes are up there," she said to no one and everybody.

"What assholes?" I asked.

"The STP Gang."

"What?" Cheryl clapped her hands to her face.

"They're living with you?" I couldn't believe that.

"No. They're squatting in the carriage house. It's like being surrounded by jackals. And little Destiny, she's freakin' out. She's afraid they'll rape her again." Georgia looked up. "I think they're gonna make a run on us."

Jewel stepped in the door. I grinned, waved. She joined me at the counter and squeezed my hand.

"Make a run on you? What's that mean?" Ed asked.

"Who knows?" Georgia said. "They're the ones with the nasty ideas. Every night they come out and start howling like crazies."

"They are the crazies," Cheryl said.

"How'd you get out?" I asked.

"I snuck out before dawn. I didn't want them to catch me." Georgia laughed. "It took me all day to get down. The snow's pretty deep."

I tried to imagine leaving the embattled Duck Lake lodge in the coldest part of that frigid night. "So, what are you guys going to do about it?" I asked.

"I don't know," she said.

"Is that why you're here?" Jewel asked. "You don't strike me as the run-and-hide type, Georgia."

"We voted. The whole family wants to hold out. Michel wants to ignore them and Bill thinks we can fight."

I groaned.

"He's impossible," Georgia said. "They both are. That's why I came. We need help."

"No shit. And you, Georgia," Cheryl said. "You're staying here."

"Maybe we should call in the sheriffs," Ed suggested.

"Last time we brought up the STP Gang," Buster said, "Boulder County Sheriff's couldn't care less."

"It's like they're protecting them," Jewel said.

"Hell, Georgia," said Buster. "Sheriff's department knows all about you and your Duck Lake squat. Have they tried to evict you? Evacuate you? Shit, no. Almost like they got a reason."

"Besides," Ed said. "It's the Sunday before Christmas. They ain't gonna be in a hurry to help us out."

"They got other reasons," Buster said. "They like it like this: One bunch of hippies chewing on another bunch of hippies."

"Can't let that happen," Cheryl said.

"No," Jewel said. "We're going to have to figure this one out for ourselves."

By the time we put together a plan, the café was full of Montgomery freaks. We had no idea how long the STP Gang was willing to play cowboys and Indians, but Georgia's story suggested we'd better hustle before the pack of frozen desperados rushed the lodge.

There was only one way to get to Duck Lake in the winter — we would have to liberate the county-owned forest fire truck, a big six-wheeled military surplus machine, built for action in WWII. It could go anywhere. Or so we hoped. Getting to Duck Lake would be next to impossible, even with the big yellow machine.

We decided to leave early that evening before Marshal Johnny got back up the canyon from Boulder. We were hijacking the county's fire truck and relations between them and Johnny were already strained. And we didn't want to broach the subject of the STP Gang or the marooned Teepee People with him. He was already pushed to the breaking point by the Sheriff's Department, his son in Vietnam. So, Ed filled us full of eggs, pancakes, and coffee to bolster us and out we went.

The early darkness brought the wind, roaring overhead like a fighter jet. Norman opened the fire shed and we cranked up the army-surplus giant, designed, built, and paid for by Boulder County to climb mountains and fight forest fires. Its original military-issue stake bed and canvas top had been replaced by a flat-welded water tank, painted bright yellow. The tank formed a deck like an aircraft carrier. On deck, a shiny, six-cylinder GMC motor sat waiting to power a water pump.

With Norman behind the wheel, we climbed Left Hand Canyon Road out of town. In the brutal weather, the eerie fluorescent light outside Ed's café looked warm and inviting. We crossed the Peak to Peak Highway and made our way onto the access road to Duck Lake. Although it hadn't been plowed, the road was easy to follow.

"It's the place where the trees ain't," Norman shouted.

The snow slashed at us and the wind whipped the tree tops, but in the forest, the roar of the engine was louder than nature. Jewel and I sat on the flat fire truck deck, back-to-back, elbows locked. We leaned into the blow and shut up. There was nothing to say and no way to say it, but her body felt warm and real behind me.

Norman clenched the wheel. If we stalled the truck up there, we'd freeze to death. Drifts slashed across roadway and Norman handled the truck like an ice breaker, plowing up and over the wind-packed drifts in a first-gear lunge, sinking down and in, backing off, and slamming into them again.

Just after dawn, we punched the big yellow truck through the Moby Dick of all snowdrifts and reached the south end of Duck Lake. Here, the forest offered no protection. We stood directly in the line of fire from the Continental Divide. Razor-sharp demons of snow raced across the bare ice. Across the lake, the lodge stood out rust-brown in the driving whiteness. My head ached from the scream of the weather harpies.

There was no sign of life at the lodge. If there was a fire going inside, it was impossible to tell. The wind would have torn the smoke off the top of the chimney before we could see it anyhow.

We left the yellow fire-fighting beast idling and struggled into the lee of the great log building. By now, we were all looking for quiet air and the comfort of a fire.

Norman pounded on the door. We heard a shout and the sound of scuffling.

"What do you want?" a male voice called.

"We want in!" I shouted.

"Fuck off, cochons!" I heard a French accent scream.

"What's that mean?" Buster shouted.

"Pigs," Malfese said. "He called us pigs."

"Michel," Jewel shouted. "It's us. We're from Montgomery. We're here to help. We don't want to hurt you."

"We're freezing out here, man," Buster shouted. "Open the goddamned door."

The door opened and Michel sized us up quickly. His eyes narrowed with suspicion as he looked past us into the bleak whiteness of the storm. He backed away and we stepped inside. Once inside, he slammed the big door and dropped a gigantic cross bar into the throats of two cast-iron brackets. The rough-hewn but elegant lobby atrium rose to windows set high in the rafters. The enormous room smelt of burnt wood and warm, sweaty bodies. The fully assembled teepee rose to the roof beams, its painted thunderheads and raccoons, bears and horses parading around the canvas circumference. Beyond the teepee a fireplace glowed and cocoons of sleeping bags huddled around the glimmer. The first-floor windows had been covered with blankets and canvas. One end of the elegant room had been filled with neatly cut and stacked firewood.

People began to stir. A child trailing a blanket stumbled out of the teepee in the serenity of half-sleep. It toddled to the fire and stared at the glowing coals.

Michel put a thick yule log on the grate. "What do you want?"

"To get you folks outta here," Norman said.

"We have no reason to leave. We have food for two months. We have firewood. We are warm. We have kerosene. We hold school for the children and we are getting into each other. You have no right to interfere with us. We are doing no harm to the place."

A number of the adults, hearing the voices, had gathered around us at the fire. They all looked somber, defiant.

"Where's Oriskany Bill?" Norman asked. "I hear tell he's been playing General What's-His-Face up here."

"He went down to town, looking for Georgia," Michel said. "He was acting crazy."

"That's a first," Jewel said sarcastically.

"Between Oriskany Bill and them weirdoes doing war dances around your campground here, looks like you got more'n your share of crazies," Norman said.

"They will go away," Michel insisted. "It's too cold for them to stick around."

"We'll put you up in town," Jewel said.

"We are not a part of your town," Michel said. "We have our own ideas about how to survive."

Several of his brothers and sisters nodded their heads in agreement.

"We have decided to stay," Michel continued. "All of us. Everybody has a voice here. Everybody. Even the children."

"Look," I said. "You've got to think bigger than that. The people who run Boulder County, they want to see us fuck up like this."

"We are not 'fucking up' as you call it," Michel sneered.

"If the Sheriff's department has to pull the STP Gang off your necks, everybody loses," I said.

"You call the Sheriff's department, that's your problem," Michel said.

"It's all our problem," I said. "The fact is, they wouldn't mind at all if the STP Gang came in here and cut all your throats. They'd be rid of two groups of undesirables."

Michel folded his arms across his chest. "We are not undesirables."

"I was trying to make a point."

"And we are not coming with you," he said.

"You've got to," I said.

"Do you have papers?" Michel asked.

"Come on, Frenchie," Buster said. "Check it out. We ain't the Man."

"Then you can't make us leave," Michel said. "I know the law."

"Get real, brother," Norman said. "Look outside." He opened the door. Blanket-clad figures were clambering onto

212

the deck of the big fire truck. They saw us and shouted. One of them started jumping up and down and grimacing. His voice was thrown away on the wind.

"Stop it!" cried a little voice.

We turned away and Norman closed the door.

Destiny, the little girl who had been raped, stood at the center of the room, wrapped in a blanket. "We're supposed to be about love and peace," she said. "But we can't. There ain't no peace here. Those people out there, that ain't no family. First of all, they don't have no girls with 'em. Girls wouldn't let this happen. They're like an army, like in the war. They don't care about life, or love, or anything. They want what we got. We better figure this out and no fighting. No shit, I'm not kidding. Or, or those people." The scrawny teenager laughed a crazy, anxious laugh and shook her head. "They'll get us all y'know."

Jewel turned to the defiant Michel. "I thought you said 'everybody,'" she said. "What about Destiny? Does she think you should all be here?"

"We better listen to Destiny, Michel," one of the other commune adults said.

"She's right," Jewel said. "Please. We all gotta get the hell out of here." She opened the door and pointed to the creatures on the fire truck. "We can't deal with these people, and neither can you."

"This is your fault," Michel shouted.

Everyone was awake and stirring. Somebody pulled a blanket off a window. It was barred from the inside with two-by-fours.

"Place looks like a fort," Malfese said.

"Give them the goddamned lodge and let's get out of here," I said.

Norman, Buster, and I ran for the truck. We would have to leave if Michel and his people refused to go quickly. Norman pulled himself on board. One of the STP Gang members started to wrestle with Norman. Buster threw him off the truck like he was a dog. Bare skin, burnt red from the cold, showed through the leather patches of his ragged blue jeans. Another figure grabbed me from behind. I pushed him away. He felt skinny and weak.

Hooting and howling, the figures stumbled off into the storm. We stood on the truck, frozen by weather and circumstance. We had to get the lodge people to leave and we had to watch the truck. We didn't dare shut off the engine. In this cold, it would never re-start, and we were using fuel just waiting there in the wind.

"We're gonna have to go back," Malfese said.

"We can't leave without them," Jewel said.

"Don't worry about it," Buster said, and nodded downwind.

The far end of the lodge blossomed with orange flame. Black smoke streamed away across the lake.

I jumped to the ground and ran towards the fire. I rounded the corner and stopped. There, huddled out of the wind was a pack of blanket-wrapped, leather-patched vandals. They were watching the fire like it was their salvation. I turned and raced for the front door. "They've torched the building," I shouted. "Now will you leave?"

Michel raced around the side of the building. The wind had fanned the flames. They were starting to lick at the eaves. His eyes widened. He ran back inside, returning with several adults carrying sticks. They ran around the corner, ready to attack. The blanket-clad figures retreated into the storm, howling like wild animals. I thought of the coyotes I had heard in town and wondered how often they had been human.

"Get your people together, Michel," I shouted over the wind. "This has gone far enough."

"We've got to put out this fire," he screamed. "The teepee . . ."

"All right," I shouted. I knew it was futile, but I had to show him we were in this together. I ran back to the truck and ground it into first gear.

"What are you doing?" Jewel shouted.

"Putting out a fire," I called back.

"You're crazy!" Buster screamed. "We won't be able to start the pump. Every nozzle is frozen. Besides, the wind is blowing that puppy completely out of control!"

"We've got to try," I said. "They'll never come with us if we don't."

Malfese slapped his forehead with a mittened hand. "Great," he said. "I'll be able to tell my grandchildren. We played fireman in a blizzard at ten thousand feet."

"To save a bunch of hippies," said Norman.

"Viva Montgomery," I shouted as we circled the end of the lodge.

Blowing at this velocity, the frigid air would supercool the engine block, making motors impossible to start. An ignition spark would do nothing in the frozen combustion chamber. You could crank the engine over until the battery went dead. But with the truck's big diesel roaring to keep the battery charged, Norman cranked the starter for the water pump's engines, feathering the choke and throttle like a concert pianist with mittens.

The pump brapped and farted into life. With both engines screaming we backed toward the fire from upwind. If the water in the tank hadn't frozen and if the hoses weren't cracked from the cold, we could pump directly onto the flames.

Putting a hose on that fire didn't do a thing. The storm took the water and flung it in a frozen spray all over the countryside.

"Like pissin' off a cliff," Norman shouted.

"Monk," I said to Malfese. "This ain't gonna happen. Get inside. Make sure those people are packed up and ready to go."

"You're gonna need diplomacy," Jewel said and joined Malfese.

I watched Jewel and Malfese push through a hip-deep snowdrift to the lodge door. I could hear the howls of the STP Gang in the forest beyond. From birdshot in Berkeley to starving feral druggies at Duck Lake. And I was going to get away from it all?

A wrong time for philosophizing. Norman and I stood on the tanker's deck, pumping water into a frozen hell. When the first of the refugees appeared on the front porch, bundled to travel, I shut down the pump. Duck Lake Lodge was a lost cause. We threw the frozen hose on board and roared up to the front door.

One by one, we pulled the communards up onto the bright yellow deck of the fire truck. Malfese and Jewel were the last to climb aboard.

"That everybody?" I shouted. Norman had the big machine in gear.

Michel counted heads and nodded.

The fire truck lurched forward.

"That's the end of that story," Malfese declared.

The communards turned backwards to look into the wind, tears frozen on their faces. I followed their eyes.

Blankets flapping in the wind, the abandoned STP denizens danced around the flaming lodge like leprechauns in a winter purgatory.

Dynamite Love

We dumped the teepee people at the community center. I built a fire in the jury-rigged potbelly and Reisinger and his wife consented to the communards using their bathroom. This was not a season for people to be dog-in-the-manger about essentials. Ed opened up the kitchen and the refugees took over the café. It wasn't exactly tourist season in the mountains.

"Gives the place a little life," Ed said.

After they ate, Jewel ushered most of the communards back down the hill to the community center to crash for the evening. Ed was cleaning up the kitchen. Georgia stayed behind and offered to help. Ed refused. "This is how I stay sane." He grinned. "There's gotta be a little order someplace."

Georgia sat down beside me. "What do you suppose'll happen to those crazies?" she asked.

"I don't know," I said. "Hopefully, they'll take shelter in whatever is left of the lodge." I looked at her, sitting with her hands folded in the lap of her dirty orange snowsuit. "You lose your stuff up there?" I asked.

She shrugged.

"You're worried about the others. They're welcome to stay until you get it together. I can clear it with Hazel."

"We can't get the bus out until spring," she said.

"It's a community center, Georgia." I looked at the huddled masses of the Teepee People. "This is what it's for. Situations like this."

"You'll figure something out," Ed said. "No hurry."

"It's not about the commune, is it?" I said.

"Sure it is." She avoided my eyes. "I'm worried about them."

"It's about you."

She shook her head.

"It can't always be about the war and other people. I'm starting to figure this out for myself. Sometimes, you got to pay attention to you. You never look inside, do you?"

She glanced up at me.

"You're like that, I can tell. You watch out for the other guy and you don't notice that your own ass . . ." I stopped.

Tears were trickling down Georgia's cheeks. She placed her head on her clasped hands. Her thick, black hair was parted in the middle.

"It's about your boyfriend. Joe." I said. "Isn't it?"

"It's my fault," she whispered, letting the sobs come openly.

Ed appeared at the table with a thick cheese sandwich and a steaming bowl of soup. "Chicken noodle," he said. "Made it myself."

"I can't pay for this," Georgia said.

"I can't pay for this either." Ed swept his arm over the café dining room. "We all got our problems," he said and disappeared into the kitchen.

"So, why your fault?"

"If I hadn't left him, he'd still be alive."

"Come on. How do you figure that?" I asked. "Joe was part of the Weather Underground," I said, testing her. "He was here to score dynamite. He . . ."

"No!" she said fiercely, eyes blazing. Georgia survived behind her ferocity. "He wanted me back, that's all. I knew he was coming." Tears made rivulets of clean on her smoky cheeks. "Well . . . I didn't know, but I could feel it." Georgia snuffled and wiped her nose with the back of a sleeve.

"Come on, woman. You could "feel" that you missed him," I said. "The rest was coincidence."

"That dynamite story," she continued. "That's bullshit. He was here to see me." She took a bite of the sandwich and looked me straight in the eye.

Oriskany Bill stormed into the café. "Hey, Georgia," he said. "Where the hell you been?" He stood by the stove in

221

the center of the room, warming his hands. "I been lookin' all over for ya," he said.

"I don't need you looking for me," she said.

Bill looked at me.

I looked at Bill and shrugged into my coat. I said goodbye to Ed, and left the café. I needed to get out of there. Georgia would have to learn how to take care of herself.

Next morning, the storm lifted. I worked outside, nailing up siding in the sunshine. Buster and Cheryl came by and took Georgia and a cluster of the displaced communards down to Boulder to look for a place to crash.

I couldn't stop thinking about what Georgia had said about her boyfriend. Her fierceness made me want to believe her. Joe wasn't here for dynamite but for love. It was possible, wasn't it? Just because he was Weather Underground, couldn't matters of the heart outweigh our days of rage? Of course they could.

But if Georgia's boyfriend died for love, who was smuggling dynamite? I didn't like the possibility that the Weather Underground was fucking things up for the Mobe. It didn't make sense and I didn't like the possibility that — even after Joe's death — the dynamite was still moving to the Bay Area from the mountains of Colorado.

Besides, Georgia's grief was real. It's tough to lie when your heart is broken. Maybe her commitment to the Teepee

People echoed the way she felt about the loss of her boyfriend. Maybe she wasn't covering a dynamite smuggler's tracks. Maybe she was mourning the loss of love and the failure of a fairy tale. She had taken on Joe and the Teepee People and she had lost them both. I knew what that felt like: to feel responsible for everybody and everything, a feeling of sacrifice that came from beneath the will, from beyond conscious memory. I was full of "maybes." I didn't know how much Georgia loved her boyfriend or the Teepee People. Speculation, I thought. Helluva way to solve a mystery. An unwanted mystery. My head ached and I wanted to talk to Jewel. She'd be able to laugh a little sense into this mess.

Rare Bitch Night

The wind came back in the late afternoon. The approaching darkness carried a knife-edged meanness. Buster and Cheryl returned from Boulder after the sun had set behind the ridge tops. They must have found a home for their load of refugees, because the truck was empty.

I stashed my tools, made sure there was a supply of firewood for the communards to keep warm in Hazel's building, and followed Norman and Buster and Cheryl up the hill. I parked at their cabin and helped them carry cardboard boxes full of groceries into the kitchen.

"Night's fixin' to be a rare bitch," Norman said, rubbing his hands together. "Hope we don't have to pull off any more high-country rescues."

"Tonight we got another agenda," Cheryl said and pulled a full bottle of Wild Turkey out of the groceries. "Good night to get loaded."

Buster grabbed four jelly glasses off the kitchen shelf. "Glad them people got a place to crash. Maybe that'll get them out of our hair."

"Man, talk about stubborn," Norman said. "We bust our asses to get up there in a damned blizzard, and them people don't want to move."

"They're safe now and besides," I said, "we got bigger fish to fry."

"Like what?" Cheryl asked.

"I just talked to Georgia. She claims her boyfriend was here looking for her. She says that whole dynamite-fetching routine is bullshit."

"I knew it didn't make sense," Norman said. "Dynamite smugglers? In Montgomery?"

The newly-stoked fire began to roar in the stove.

"Besides," Norman continued, "the sheriff's department hasn't done shit about it."

"They'd love to pin a smuggling rap on us," Cheryl said.

"It'd go a long way in their clean-up-the-mountains crusade." I stopped. "Maybe I'm just paranoid."

"Paranoia's good for ya." Buster took a big swig of bourbon.

"Boyfriend or no, somebody's still blowing up power poles in California," I said.

"And your alleged dynamite smuggler has been dead for months," Buster said.

"So who wants to blow up power poles?" Cheryl asked. The little cabin had grown dark. We were all sitting around the kitchen table, facing the glow of the stove.

"You know," I continued, "after we put the community center fire out . . ."

"Been a lotta fires around here," Buster said.

"I went down to tell Hazel. She didn't get upset or anything. She just patted me on the knee and looked up the word 'fire' in the dictionary.

"Weird," Cheryl said.

"Big dictionary," I continued. "Lot of meanings. One of them stuck in my head. It used the word "fire" in something called the letters of fire and sword. It was an old meaning, like from the sixteen hundreds, from Scotland. 'Letters of fire and sword' allowed the local sheriff to kick out an obstinate tenant. By any means necessary. Including torching the joint."

"You think somebody looked up a three-hundred year-old phrase and used it on us?" Cheryl asked. "You really are paranoid."

"No, no," I said. "I don't think anybody in the Boulder Sheriff's Department is getting ideas out of the dictionary. But whoever torched Hazel's building . . . might have done it in the name of the state."

"Kinda like that old English guy," Buster said.

"Guy Fawkes," Norman said.

"Carl said the same thing," I said.

Norman and Buster looked at each other, eyebrows raised. "You been talkin' to Carl again?" Norman asked.

"Hey, guys . . ." Cheryl pointed to the window. "Forget about Carl Matthews."

Outside, a forlorn strip of red sunset had opened beneath the leaden clouds. Against the gray sky and the barren hillside, a determined little figure in a dirty orange snowsuit stepped away from Jewel's cabin and began climbing the hill against the wind. Georgia.

"Okay, she just left Jewel's. So now where's she going?" Cheryl asked.

"Just watch." Norman turned away from the window and poured himself another jelly glass of Wild Turkey. "In this town, you'll find out quick enough."

Norman was right. We could follow every move Georgia made in the fishbowl of Montgomery's cabins and switchback roads.

"It's Brucie," Buster said. "She's headed for Brucie's."

"Jesus," Norman said. "I hope she ain't lookin' for shelter from the storm up there."

"I'm gonna go talk to Jewel." I pulled on my coat. "See what Georgia wanted."

I opened the door. The wind pulled it out of my hands and slammed it against the outside cabin wall. The darkening world felt like outer space. I had to force the frozen, fast-moving air down my lungs, but I struck out for Jewel's place. I was curious about Georgia. I wanted to believe her story about Joe DeStephano, dedicated politico and broken-hearted boyfriend.

A Bloody Ear

I knocked on Jewel's door and stood my ground against the wind. The porch roof rattled against its moorings, poised to rocket away on the storm. Jewel opened up immediately. You don't let people stand outside for long in weather like that.

"Well, well." She chuckled. "Visitors galore." She pulled me inside the yellow warmth of her kitchen. "Seeking shelter?" she asked. "Any port in a storm?"

"I'll ignore the wisecracks," I replied.

"They're not wisecracks," she said. "They're innuendo. And you're not supposed to ignore them." She motioned me to sit down. "So, what brings a dog like you out on a night like this?" She moved a smoke-stained kettle onto the burner.

"I'm curious about Georgia," I said. "What's going on with her?"

"Georgia?" Jewel asked, raising one eyebrow. "Our nights of bliss haven't driven every other woman from your heart?" Jewel looked at me sideways. "Cup of tea?"

"Sure" I replied. "Can I ask the questions now?"

"Blunt," Jewel replied. "But effective. Fire away, sailor."

"What did she want here?" I asked.

Jewel shrugged. "Shelter from the storm."

"Come on," I prodded. "What's going on with her? If it makes any difference, I'm not inquiring for personal reasons. She may standing in the middle of a landslide that could bury the whole town."

"Colorful." Jewel poked another piñon log onto the fire and straddled her chair, tea pot in one hand, cups in another, and a half-pint of brandy hooked under her little finger. "She is pretty broke up about her old man." Jewel looked up sharply at me. "You can relate to that, can't you? That she misses her old man?"

"Sure," I replied, dodging more attitude.

"She talked about getting stuck up there at Duck Lake with that crazy guy."

"Oriskany Bill."

"The same." She dropped a dose of brandy into her tea. "She wanted to talk about her real boyfriend. She wants to figure out what happened to him."

"Her dead boyfriend."

"She thinks Brucie knows something about it."

"Juicy Brucie Berenger?" That didn't make sense. "What would Brucie know about a dead body in the National Forest?"

"Dunno." Jewel took a sip of her tea. "She wouldn't say."

"Georgia wants to talk but there's something she isn't telling you."

Something like that. But she talked about Brucie in the same breath with her dead boyfriend as you so eloquently put it."

"And Georgia says her dead boyfriend was here in Montgomery to see her."

"Right." Jewel handed me the hot mug. "Not smuggling dynamite."

"Okay." I took a slug. "I believe her. Sure, this guy was part of the Weather Underground but they can fall in love, too."

"I would imagine," Jewel said. "You know, revolutionaries get guided by great feelings of love . . ."

"Che Guevara." We both said it at once.

"But back to Weather Underground," I said. "They're very careful about where they plant their bombs. And I know a little bit about what's happening in Port Chicago."

"Port Chicago?"

"Where the dynamite showed up. Port Chicago is a Navy munitions depot north of San Francisco. They load bombs and shit onto ships bound for Vietnam. There's been a lot of demonstrations up there — organized by the Mobe."

"The Mobe," Jewel repeated. "Like the whale, I suppose."

"Like the Mobilization to End the War in Vietnam."

"Where do you get this shit, Sherlock?" Jewel asked.

"From the people who bring you the antiwar movement. You do know there is a war going on, right? And that there's a movement against the war, que no?"

"I'll ignore that," Jewel poured another shot into her tea. "So, how does Port Whatever hook up with Juicy pitiful Brucie and the price of dynamite in Colorado?"

"Why would the Weather Underground or the Mobe want to short out the power in a place they're trying to get friendly with?"

"Come again?" Jewel asked.

"Power poles. Why would they blow up the electricity? That just fucks with everyday people. They're taking on the U.S. military up there — in wartime. It'd be stupid to pick a fight with the whole community. And cutting off the electricity sure as hell doesn't stop the Man from shipping ammo out of the harbor. They know that."

"So?"

"So that leaves one alternative. Agents provocateurs."

"Like spies?"

"Government trouble-makers. Like any anti-war demo that goes sour. Cops start most of the riots, pigs in hippie garb, fucking things up. Agents provocateurs."

"Boy," Jewel said, her eyes gleaming at me over the rim of her tea cup. "For a guy who's trying to get away from it all, you sure think a lot."

"Problem is . . . I know too much."

"Well, smell you!" She laughed. "Must be rough being such an expert."

"Yeah. I'm supposed to be up here letting the wind blow through my ears but all this shit keeps comin' down."

"Baby boy." She put a hand on my arm. "If you didn't want to mess with this story, you wouldn't."

"It's tough to drop out when you been shot in the ass by a bunch of shotgun-wielding pigs."

"Pigs with guns. A cute image. Little pink snouts. Shotguns." Jewel put her arms around me and caressed my buttocks. "How's your ass now?"

"Feels fine." Her touch sent warm waves through me despite the wind and the chaos.

"Good," she said. "I went to New Mexico." She nuzzled my neck. "Not that you asked. It was cold there, too." She smelled of wood smoke and soap. "It's nice to be back."

Blam, blam, blam.

Jewel sighed and opened the door. The storm rushed in like an angry bully, blowing Buster and Cheryl inside.

"New and revolting developments," Cheryl announced.

"Oriskany Bill's on the warpath," Buster said. "He wants his lady back."

"Georgia?" Jewel asked. "His 'lady?' First off, he's delusional. Georgia isn't anybody's 'lady.' Second, Georgia thinks Oriskany Bill is an asshole."

"Bingo," Cheryl glared at her husband. "But that isn't the point. Buster let it slip that Georgia was over at Juicy Brucie's."

Jewel groaned.

Cheryl gave Buster a cuff behind the ear with the sleeve of her jacket.

"Fuck it," Buster growled. "Let 'em sort this thing out on their own."

"Oriskany Bill and Juicy Brucie in the same cabin with Georgia?" I asked.

"Yep."

I whistled softly.

"Norman went to roust Johnny," Buster added.

"We better not wait for that," I said.

Jewel grabbed her boots. "I'll go with you."

We stepped outside, the howling wind surrounding us again like wolves. It never fell off its crescendo. Unrelenting wind like that makes your hair stand on end. It makes you gnash your teeth, makes you want to punch somebody.

As we clambered uphill toward Brucie's, Malfese bolted down Modoc Street. The wind at his back lengthened his strides as if he was walking on the moon. He raised his hand and shouted but his words blew past us in attenuated fragments.

"Fuck, man," Malfese exploded when he reached us. "Weirdest thing I ever seen. I thought Oriskany Bill was camped out at the community center."

"He was," I said.

"Not anymore!" Malfese braced himself against the wind. "I just seen him take off up the hill!"

"Where was he coming from?" Cheryl asked.

"Looked like he was over at Juicy Brucie's. Shit, it's goddamn cold!" Malfese exploded. "Let's get out of this wind."

We made it into the lee of Brucie's front porch. Kerosene light glowed from the kitchen but the rest of the cabin lay in darkness. We heard a scream and burst through the front door.

Inside, the kitchen was in a shambles. The table was overturned, a chair lay face down, its back broken. Coffee cups, a bottle of whiskey, and a shattered kerosene lantern littered the linoleum.

Georgia lay curled on the floor, one wrist handcuffed to the grill of Brucie's cook stove.

"He's in the other room," Georgia whispered.

"Where's Oriskany?" I asked.

"He took off," she said.

I moved past Georgia to peer into the murky darkness of Brucie's bedroom. A bearded figure hunched over on the bedside, rocking back and forth and groaning.

"Brucie! You okay?" All I got in response were more groans.

"Tell him to give us the key!" Buster shouted from the kitchen.

"Come on, Brucie." I grabbed his left arm and pulled him off the bed. "What's the deal with the handcu . . .?" I stared.

Brucie was holding the sheet up to his right ear. It was covered in blood.

"What happened to your face, man?"

"What's it look like, asshole?" Brucie glared at me, teeth clenched in pain. "That big fucker chopped my ear off!" He stood, head bowed, bobbing and weaving with pain and dizziness.

"Who? Oriskany?"

"Who do you think," Brucie muttered.

I looked around the darkened bedroom. No key to be found. I shoved him back onto the bed.

The wind screamed under the eaves.

"Where's the key, Brucie?"

He moaned.

I grabbed him by the shoulders and shook him. "The key, motherfucker!"

He screamed.

"Buster, Cheryl!" I hollered. "Gonna need a little persuasion in here."

"Find it yourself," he said. "I put it on the kitchen table before that maniac jumped me."

I returned to the light in the kitchen.

Jewel had found the key on the kitchen floor and was twisting it in the handcuff. Georgia gave a tight scream of rage as the lock snapped open. She dragged the chair away from the stove and sat down heavily, rubbing her wrist.

Jewel knelt next to her. "What happened?"

"I came up here to talk to Brucie." Georgia jerked her head toward the bedroom. "About Joe. My boyfriend." Disgust floated across Georgia's dark features. "He knows. He knows what happened." The wind bellowed against the flimsy walls of the cabin. "Then I started asking questions."

"Like what kind of questions?" I asked.

"Like how come Brucie lives here now."

"What does that mean?" I asked.

"It means I know this Brucie guy from other places," she said.

"Like where?" Cheryl asked.

"Jesus, Joseph, and Mary!" Malfese exclaimed and went down to one knee. He picked something off the littered linoleum and held it up to the light. It was an ear. Malfese's eyes turned up in his head and he crumpled to the floor.

Jewel turned wide-eyed towards Georgia. "Did you do that?"

Georgia shook her head. "Bill did it," she said.

"That was somebody's ear," Malfese said and rubbed his face.

Cheryl stepped over the Monk's legs and opened the kitchen door, the wind beast filling the room. She brought a handful of snow into the house, grabbed a blue enameled coffee cup, and packed it with snow. Gingerly, she lifted the ear from the floor and deposited it in the cup. Blood stained the crystalline whiteness with crimson. The blood and snow glistened sharp-edged and clean against the blue enameled cup. Nurse Cheryl had rescued an ear.

Fists pounded on the door. "Open up! Open up in there!"

Buster slipped the latch and Johnny LaPorte stepped into Brucie's kitchen. Norman Bowkers, clad in a hooded Navy anorak, filled the rest of the available space.

Johnny looked around the room. "Mother of Christ."

Georgia sat in the corner rubbing her recently handcuffed wrist. A broken chair leaned against the table. The tin cup containing Brucie's ear sat on the kitchen counter. Malfese sat, legs splayed out on the floor like an emaciated Rasputin.

"What in hell's name are you people up to now?" Johnny asked weakly.

Silence. We were too stunned to come up with an explanation.

Brucie staggered to the kitchen doorway, trailing the bloody sheet behind him like a security blanket.

"Christmas!" Johnny said.

Brucie was too far gone to talk. He gave a yowl and fell back into his room.

Johnny followed him in, dragged the sheet away from Brucie's wound and looked long and hard.

"Jesus," he said.

The wind hit the corner of the cabin with a solid whack.

"Bring a light in here." Johnny stared at the side of Brucie's face. "Well, you'll live," Johnny proclaimed. "But you're gonna need a new ear."

"We got one. In the kitchen," Malfese offered as he peered into the crowded bedroom.

Brucie started to babble. "That Oriskany Bill guy did it." His nose was full of snot like a kid who'd been crying for a long time. "And he killed that guy up in the woods." He nodded towards Georgia. "Her boyfriend! The dynamite smuggler," he said. He kept his eyes on the floor, like a dog that had just been whacked. "He was scared Georgia was gonna leave. He was jealous."

"That's a lie," Georgia said calmly.

241

Brucie turned back to Johnny. "She's one of 'em, you know — the dynamite smugglers. I figure she's the one who knows the suppliers. She was the contact for her boyfriend."

"My old man wasn't here to smuggle dynamite. He was here to see me," Georgia said simply.

"Call the sheriff," Brucie spat.

Johnny grabbed Brucie by the collar. "Listen, you little fuck," he said. "Don't you tell me what to do."

"I'm bleedin' to death here," Brucie wailed, holding the bloody sheet away from his mangled ear for emphasis.

"The hell you are," Johnny replied. "And I'm not callin' anybody until I can make sense out of this!"

"You got your Bronco right out there," Brucie wailed. "Why don't you call a doctor?"

"You don't have to use your radio, Marshal. You can call the Boulder County Sheriff's Department from here."

Johnny spun around.

Georgia stood at the end of the bed, arms folded across her chest. "He's got a radio right in there." She nodded toward the closet door.

I opened the closet door. Sitting on the shelf above the clutter of Brucie's clothes was a short-wave Hallicrafters radio and a nasty-looking black dispatcher's microphone. The green light from the wave-band gauge cast an eerie glow into the room.

Georgia continued talking in a dead-flat monotone. "When I came up here, he was using that thing. Talking to the sheriff's department. I heard the radio squawking so I stopped and listened from outside. It was him." Georgia jerked her head toward Brucie. "He was talking about me. And my boyfriend. And this stupid dynamite smuggling thing. Sounded like they had talked about it before. I went in to stop him. He grabbed me. That's when he handcuffed me to the stove. Said he was going to have me arrested. Then Bill busted through the door."

"That Bill fella? Ain't he your boyfriend?" Johnny asked.

Georgia gave a little laugh. She had a sad, ancient look on her face, the look of a woman who has — once again — been tagged as the whore of Babylon. Her story-telling was over.

Johnny crossed the little room in two steps. He shut down the Hallicrafters radio, yanked the microphone cord out of its socket, and stuffed the mike in his parka pocket. He motioned us to follow him outside.

"What about Brucie?" Cheryl asked.

"He'll stay put." Johnny stepped to the lee side of Brucie's cabin. He glared at us in the luminous darkness. "I'm going to start talking," he said. "Anybody knows anything I don't know, speak up. Clear enough?" He looked around.

We huddled against the cold and listened.

"We got a murder. We got a building burnt right here in town for no good reason. Duck Lake gets habitated by a bunch of gangsters, right behind my back, the lodge goes up in flames. And now . . ." Johnny pointed his pipe at the front door. "We got more Boulder County bad medicine sittin' in there holdin' the side of his head."

"If they can prove somebody was smuggling dynamite out of Montgomery and across state lines," I shouted over the wind, "the County can pretty much sink this little town."

Johnny nodded. "Interstate violation. Federal rap. Conspiracy to commit treason. Big trouble." He lit his pipe upside down in the wind, like a sailor. "One thing for sure," he said. "This guy with the ear . . ." Johnny poked the air with his pipe. "Talkin' to Boulder County behind my back. That makes him a sneak. And a spy. And Boulder County's been eatin' it up. That short wave radio in there, that's County property. They been aidin' and abettin' this little snitch. They got some explainin' to do. And you know damned well," he added. "He radio'd them when you folks dragged that body down from the forest. Before anybody else knew about it. Him and his goddamned shortwave." Johnny paused for a moment. "I got caught with my pants down one time." He gazed out over the tiny town. "I won't get fooled again."

Georgia reached into her parka and brought out a tightly wound roll of money. "I found this in his kitchen drawer."

"That's Hazel's money," I said. "Or what's left of it. He stole it, not Sullivan. Right out of my truck. This guy has been messing with everybody."

A violent gust swept the porch.

I slammed through Brucie's cabin door, grabbed the snow-filled cup that cradled the ear, strode into the bedroom and thrust the cup in Brucie's face.

He grabbed for the half-frozen appendage, then sunk back onto the bed, faint with the effort.

I walked over to the stove and opened the firebox door. The coals glowed cherry-red in the kerosene light.

"Okay, motherfucker," I choked out. "You want to see your ear again? Start talking."

"What are you doin' in there?" Johnny hollered.

"Gimme a minute with this guy," I said.

They must have taken me seriously. No one stirred.

I held the ear in its bowl near the open door of the stove. An ember popped. "Start talking," I said, evenly.

"About what?" Brucie asked. His face was white as a sheet.

"You stole the money."

"What money?"

"Hazel's money. Out of the glove compartment of my truck. This money." I thrust the wad of money in his face.

Brucie looked away.

Johnny edged into the room and stood by the door, arms folded.

"You torched the community center, didn't you? You listened to me and Reisinger bullshit you about stovepipe and the hazards of fire and you went in there and burnt us out. Didn't you!"

Brucie's silence cemented my suspicions.

"And you weren't just talking about the weather to those deputies up at the café that day." I turned to Johnny. "He was talkin' to that guy Rowdy . . ."

"And that other deputy," Buster added. "Roy."

"I know 'em both," Johnny gestured Buster out of the room.

I turned back to Brucie. "Right after that, those County pigs rousted me for my draft card. They told me somebody from Montgomery was smuggling dynamite. Remember that?" Still cradling his amputated ear, I spat into the open door of the stove and turned back to Brucie. "You work for Boulder County, right, Brucie?" I spoke slowly and deliberately, struggling to keep my anger from quivering my voice. "You're a snitch. You called ahead about the body in the forest." I could hear my voice rise above the storm. "Your pig friends down in Boulder, they didn't want to bust the STP Gang. They knew the STP Gang was causing all kinds of mayhem up here. They told you to turn up the wick, so you torched Hazel's building," I shouted. "Didn't you, you little creep. Didn't you! You and the Boulder County Sheriff's Department, you're real tight."

Brucie stared up at me, belligerent. I wanted to grab him, shake him until he bled again.

"Speak of the devil," Buster called from the window. "Sheriffs 're comin' up Left-Hand Canyon Road. A bunch of 'em."

I grabbed Brucie. "Get up," I said. "They aren't gonna bail you out this time, snitch."

"Hold it, Gus," Johnny said. "We got the law to answer to here."

"The law. They're in on this, Johnny," I said. "They're trying to make this town look like shit. We give them Brucie now, they'll just stack it up against us. They're the Man. So's he. I've seen it before, creeps like this guy. They don't know which side they're on. They're ready to talk to anybody."

Johnny must have caught the rage in my eyes. "Go on, then. Do your thing," he said. "Get him outta here and we'll buy you some time." He stepped back into the kitchen.

I pulled Brucie to his feet and tossed him a towel to stop the flow of blood.

I tossed Brucie his parka and yanked open the back door. As an afterthought, I ran back into the bedroom, pulled the ear out of the snow-filled cup, wrapped it in a sock, and thrust it into my jacket pocket.

In the kitchen, Johnny shaped up his posse. "Okay, people," he said. "We got to entertain these Boulder deputies for a quick minute while Gus plays back door man with our friend here. Nobody has the slightest idea where these two went. Get it? Not a word."

The deputies pounded on the door.

Brucie took a breath to shout for help.

I muffled him. "Shut up or I'll strangle you," I growled from a depth I didn't recognize.

Brucie believed me. He remained silent.

A second Sheriff's vehicle pulled up.

I kicked my captive into the windy darkness and hauled him up the hill. We crouched behind Hazel's building and waited while a third sheriff's vehicle drove silently through town, headed toward the café.

"You guys were planning a big party tonight," I said. "Weren't you?"

Brucie said nothing.

Enough, I thought. I was going to scare the shit out of Brucie the snitch. I dragged him across the road and pushed him into the Odd Fellow's Hall.

"What're you doing?" he whimpered. "Are you crazy?"

"Yeah." I stood in the big room, waiting for my eyes to adjust to the darkness.

The big structure groaned in the wind.

"There's a guy I want you to meet." I grabbed Brucie by the collar and pulled him up the stairs.

He began whining. "I didn't do nothin'," he gasped.

"Right now, motherfucker," I hissed at Brucie, "everything you do and say . . ." I gave his collar an extra tug for emphasis, "Matters." I hoped I would find Carl there. I wanted to give this guy a heart attack.

"What the hell you got there, Beelzebub?" Carl hollered down the stairs. My rapport with the old miner was going to work in my favor.

"Now you're in the company of the devil," I told Brucie.

At the top of the stairs, dim light from the outdoors shone through the single window, illuminating the tall rafters and lofty peak of the Odd Fellows' Hall. My hostage tripped over one of the bentwood chairs.

I let him sprawl. "Oops," I said and hauled him to his feet in front of Carl.

"Looks like he's had one helluva night so far," Carl said from his chair. He raised his voice to address Brucie. "Jaysus. How the hell'd you lose your ear?"

Brucie didn't answer.

"Sit down, snitch." I sat Brucie down in a chair and turned to Carl. "This guy's been tellin' lies to just about everybody," I said. "He's been living amongst us, setting us up. He burnt down Hazel's building."

Carl said nothing.

"What do you want with me?" Brucie asked.

"You and me," I continued. "We know things that other people around here don't know. Right?"

Brucie shrugged and shivered in the dark.

"About dynamite smugglers. About a dead guy you knew from before." I laughed. "Not exactly an old friend, fuckface?"

"What do you say, Carl?" I wanted chain rattling.

Silence.

Fuck it, I thought. *I'll rattle the chains myself.* I turned back to Brucie. "So you stole Hazel's money. And you set fire to Hazel's building, didn't you?" I shook him. "Didn't you!"

Brucie nodded.

"Why?" I asked.

"They told me to," he said.

"Who?

"Boulder County. The sheriff."

"Why?"

"They're trying to make it tough for you people. They want to get rid of you."

I turned to Carl. "You get the picture. Give me a hand."

Carl gave me a hand, a round of applause, then laughed at his own joke. The laugh decayed into a phlegmatic wheeze.

"Wh-wh-who you talkin' to?" Brucie asked.

Carl sat silently in his chair.

I shook Brucie again. "Talk to me about dynamite. What do you know about dynamite?"

Red light flashed on the loft windows. Below me, three Boulder County Sheriff's vehicles clustered around Brucie's cabin. They looked tiny, insignificant. I felt strangely secure in my lofty perch as if Brucie and I were in sanctuary.

"Can I have my ear back?" Brucie whined.

" 'Can I have my ear back?' " I mocked him. "You sound ridiculous." I stood over him, clamping his arm in a claw-like grip.

"Give the kid his ear back," Carl said.

"Look," I said. "This guy has been messing with us."

"He's a pathetic little snitch," Carl said. "Nothin' new in that."

"He burnt my building down."

"So, you got him shittin' in his pants," he said. "What's that gonna get ya?"

"There's also a dead guy that didn't have to get dead, Carl."

"Yeah, well... So's your old man," he growled, and spat on the floor.

Brucie stared at me like he'd seen a ghost.

"You heard me," Carl said. "So's your old man."

"My old man's already dead."

"Not the way I read it. You're lookin' to kill somebody. Might be your old man, right?"

"Wrong. The sonofabitch beat me to the punch," I said. The image of my father, hanging from the overhead pipes in the windowless cinderblock bunker of his university lab flashed through my brain like a strobe. "That's got nothing to do with it," I said.

"Life's fulla surprises, ain't it, Beelzebub?" Carl snorted. "Your old man kills himself and the whole world goes upside down. This poor fool's the one got nothin' to do with it," he said.

"That's where you're wrong," I said. I turned back to Brucie.

"You're fuckin' crazy," Brucie said.

I shook Brucie until his teeth rattled. "The dynamite. Where does it come from?"

Brucie glared up at me.

Carl sat silently in his chair, hands poised, fingertip to fingertip, judging me.

I was alone. No one could help me. I pulled the sock with Brucie's ear out of my parka pocket. I felt cold inside. Cold and confident. I was going to make this motherfucker talk. "Come on, you little prick. Where are you getting the dynamite? I'm all ears."

"All ears." Carl cracked up. "Not hardly."

I walked to the window and looked out.

"Silver Hill," Brucie hissed. "I get it from a couple of guys in Silver Hill."

An image of the drugstore cowboys at Buster's stag party flashed into my head. I remembered the warmth and the firelight at the Silver Hill Inn and the incongruous, angry words about Montgomery.

"What kind of bullshit is that?" I shouted. "Who gets the dynamite? Come on Brucie!" I spun the sock overhead, whirring, whirring, like a rotor.

"All right!" he shouted back. "It's for some guys out near Port Chicago. I have to do it!"

"We all got our place in the world, shithead," I said. "What guys?"

"Just guys, that's all. They work for the FBI."

"CointelPro."

"Yeah, CointelPro. I have to do it, otherwise, I go to jail." His eyes gleamed in the darkness. "Get it?" He glared at me. "You crazy-ass freak."

"Sticks and stones, motherfucker. Tell the truth." I said.

Down at Brucie's I could see a crowd of hippies, bundled against the wind surrounding the Sheriffs' vehicles. The Teepee People. They were singing and swaying together in the darkness.

One by one, the big pig Blazers turned around, pushed through the little mob of hippies, and headed back down the canyon. The numbers on their roofs shone black on white as they drove beneath my hideout.

"There go your buddies, shithead," I told Brucie. "They can't help you now. It's time to go back and tell Johnny and your neighbors what you just told me."

I pulled Brucie out of his seat. He wobbled bewildered, childish, holding the towel to the stub of his ear "Who was that you were talking to?"

"Who . . . him?" I turned around. Carl was nowhere to be seen but his coffee cup sat on the floor gleaming like a jawbone in the pale light from the window.

"He prefers to remain anonymous." I pushed Brucie toward the stairs and shouted back at the empty loft. "Thanks for nothing, Carl."

Back in Brucie's cabin, Johnny and the Montgomery sleuth group listened to the new juice from Brucie. "He says it's CointelPro," I said. "They're the ones blowing up power poles in Port Chicago."

"Tell me more," Johnny said.

"CointelPro is the FBI's counterintelligence unit," I said. "They got snitches and trouble-makers planted all over the antiwar movement. Most of them are weasels like this guy. Snitching for a deal against jail time." I dropped Brucie's ear back in the cup.

"Ecch," Cheryl said.

I felt as if I was hanging upside down by one ankle. Something had broken loose inside. All my anger had turned to sorrow. My old man was gone. He didn't live inside me anymore. He had stepped onto a gallows of his own making. He had executed himself. Capital punishment. Who was the judge? Not me. What had been the crime? Not mine.

Without him inside, my head had filled with new questions and my heart was full of hot sorrowful dust. Had I become a revolutionary to vent my anger? Was the revolution just the fear of a boy who had lost his father? The questions crowded around me. I was amazed I hadn't understood this all before. But I knew the world was real and only half lay inside my head. I wasn't going to fall apart. Not now. I turned my attention back to Brucie.

"According to our friend here, this mess works both ways. The antiwar people, they're trying to stop the weapons shipments that leave Port Chicago, headed for Vietnam. But they aren't into sabotage. Now the Weathermen, they believe in change — by any means necessary. But they wouldn't double-cross the antiwar people. They come from the same place."

"You lost me," Johnny said.

"Brucie works both sides of the street," I said. "He works with the Boulder County Sheriffs to make Montgomery look bad . . ."

"We are bad, man," Malfese boasted.

Johnny watched me closely. He wasn't convinced.

"This dynamite smuggling thing turns into good propaganda for the Man," I said. "People in Boulder County think we're bombers. That makes Montgomery look like a bandit's nest. People in California don't know the feds are planting the dynamite. They think the protestors are cutting off power to homes, hospitals, schools. That makes the antiwar movement look like scum. And CointelPro gets to use the dynamite to make it all happen."

Brucie laughed. "He's nuts," he said. "He talks to people who aren't there."

"Shut up." Johnny said.

"Up there, in that warehouse," Brucie said. "He kept talking to some guy." He sneered. "There was nobody there."

"What makes you so sure about that?" Norman asked. "I happen to be personally acquainted with that nobody. Goes by the name of Carl." He chuckled. "Salty old fucker."

"Carl," Johnny said. "He's back in town?"

"One and the same," Norman said. "Gus has been talkin' with him lately. Seems old Carl's up to his usual tricks."

Brucie looked from Norman to Johnny, wide-eyed. "You guys better get me to a hospital," he moaned.

Johnny put his boot on Brucie's bedside. "I can tell you, son, if those boys in Boulder find out you been smuggling dynamite under their noses, they're gonna think twice about bailing you out."

"I got the federal government behind me," Brucie said. "Anything happens to me . . ."

"I wouldn't waste a minute getting rough with you," Johnny said. "You're not worth the trouble. You're going to the hospital and then to jail. In that order. Your federal friends can decide for themselves whether to save your worthless butt or throw you in the slammer for transporting explosives across state lines. And you can take your goddamned ear with ya."

"I didn't smuggle any of it."

"Conspiracy, son," Johnny said. "Conspiracy to transport." He turned to Brucie. "I want to see which road they'll take. Playing dumb about all this malarkey and throwing you to the dogs or protectin' your sorry ass." Johnny stood. "I'll take him down the hill. We're about done here"

"No. We're not done here."

Heads spun.

Georgia approached the bed and looked down at Brucie. "Ask him about my boyfriend."

"Huh?" Johnny had sucked in enough information for the evening.

"If this creep is the one smuggling the dynamite . . ." What was my boyfriend doing here?" Georgia asked.

"How the hell do I know?" Brucie whined.

"Oh yes, you do," Georgia said. "My boyfriend fingered you. He knew you were a snitch."

"You know this woman?" Johnny asked.

The room went dead. Even the wind seemed to catch its breath.

"I remember you now," Georgia whispered. "You came to the antiwar office in Oakland."

Brucie didn't move a muscle.

Johnny loomed over Brucie. "The quicker you tell me what's goin' on — all of it — the quicker you're gonna get to the hospital," Johnny said.

Brucie expelled a long breath. He pointed to Georgia. "Her boyfriend, Joe. He came into the Silver Hill Inn one afternoon," Brucie said. "I was there, talking business. He was looking for her."

"What kind of business?" I asked. "Tell them what you told me, up at the Odd Fellows' Hall."

"They had more dynamite," Brucie said. "They wanted to unload it. I had the money from the feds . . ."

"What did you do to my boyfriend?" Georgia demanded.

"He recognized me. From that peace-creep office in Oakland."

"So you killed him." Georgia jumped on Brucie. She pummeled him on the shoulders, the back, anywhere she could land a fist.

"No! No!" Brucie dropped to the floor. "I didn't do it.

Johnny pulled Georgia off him. "They did! They killed him. Those guys at the Silver Hill Inn! The guys who picked up the dynamite."

"Bunch of sheriff's deputies hang out there," Johnny said.

"They were just supposed to scare him," Brucie whined. "They took Joe up to the forest. I don't know what went wrong. I wasn't there. They just told me they took care of him."

"And you didn't ask any questions," I said.

"Hey," Brucie said, his lips twisted in a contemptuous curl, "what you don't know can't hurt you."

Georgia screamed and attacked again. Johnny dragged the grief-stricken woman off Brucie.

"I told you!" she sobbed. "It wasn't about dynamite or the war or anything!" Her sadness rose into a wail that fought the wind for its fury. "He was just looking for me!"

Johnny packed Brucie and his ear into the back seat of the Bronco and handcuffed him to the door. He wanted Georgia to ride down to Boulder but she refused to ride in the same vehicle with the man who had been responsible for the death of her lover. Instead, she rode sandwiched like a child between Buster and Cheryl in their pickup. I watched the tiny caravan drive off into the darkness. Then I walked home, shut the door, and built a fire against the storm outside.

That night, sleeping alone in the still cold air of my mountain cabin, I dreamt about my father for the first time since he died. I was in my Chevy pickup, climbing a spiral road, circling a bright mountain that rose out of the Great Plains. The air sparkled and a clear, animated creek bubbled over polished stones. My foot to the floor, I broadsided the truck into every turn, steering on full opposite lock. Despite the speed and momentum of my broadsides, I could make out every branch and stone, every pine needle and cone. Even the beer cans by the side of the road stood out in exquisite detail. My vision extended everywhere.

When I reached the mountaintop, I found a circle of cabins forming a ring around the peak. I was welcomed by the townspeople who brought me to a cabin that was to be mine for as long as I wanted it. Woolly and Zoom were with me. They went running off to explore the new village. My father was dressed in a white maritime uniform and his blonde hair blew in the perfect wind. Bolts of lightning were embroidered on the mortar boards at his shoulders, the insignia for Sparks, the ever-present moniker for a radio operator at sea. He lay a hand on my shoulder. "I wanted to show you the world," he said. "How it worked, what was beautiful but my wiring short-circuited. When I looked at you, I knew I was too crazy to be anybody's old man. But those were my monsters, not yours. You don't have to take them on. I'm all right now. And so are you."

VERNAL EQUINOX

The wind stopped the next morning. Nobody noticed it at first, but when they finally heard the silence, people walked out into the warm, still air and raised their faces to the sky. That night, in the light of a waning moon, Norman snowshoed back through the quiet forest to re-inhabit his cabin. He found Oriskany Bill inside, huddled under a pile of blankets and wrapped around Norman's personal supply of 150-proof Wild Turkey. He was crying for his kids back in Florida.

Norman rousted Bill, filled him full of coffee, bread, bacon, and beans and dragged him down to the bus station in Boulder. He gave the self-proclaimed outlaw $50 and thanked him for performing a civic duty. "After all," he reasoned later, "if Bill hadn't come stormin' into Brucie's place with a big attitude and a bowie knife, we never would have pried that little weasel out from under his rock." Civic duty or not, Norman made damned sure Oriskany Bill was safely installed on a bus heading East before he drove back up the mountain.

Juicy Brucie and the boys from Silver Hill never got charged for smuggling the dynamite but they couldn't sew Brucie's ear back on. Somewhere, a one-eared weasel still has to explain what happened to the side of his face. I'm sure he's lying about it.

Nobody got arrested for the murder of Georgia's boyfriend. He became another casualty of the war at home, joining a list of civil rights workers and war resisters, red, black, brown and white, who were killed by police, the feds, and by the trapped young draftees in the National Guard.

Jewel and I never did get back together. After Brucie lost his ear, she headed for school in North Carolina. She had decided she wanted to become a therapist and shrink people's heads. "If people weren't so crazy," she reasoned, "maybe they wouldn't be so quick to pick fights with little yellow people in foreign lands." She kissed me long and soft, looked into my eyes, and laughed. "The course of lust never runs true," she said and left without a backward glance.

I finished the community center — again. We threw another big party and nobody burned the place down. Hazel was delighted that I had salvaged her commercial property. She sat through the party with a generous, mischievous glint in her eye. At one point she drew me to her side. "To submit to the severest ordeal or proof, to encounter or face the greatest dangers or hardest chances," she said.

When I asked her where the quote came from, Hazel looked at me as if I should be ashamed. "Why the Oxford English Dictionary, of course," she said. "Part of our definition of fire."

Carl Matthews never did reappear. Norman and Jim did their best to convince me he was a ghost, but the sound of his voice and his cough were too clear. His uncanny ability to grouse about my thoughts and feelings did seem like a supernatural thing but many mysteries are better left untouched. That way, you don't need a god to explain everything for you.

On the first day of spring I brewed up a pot of coffee, swept the cabin, and banked the stove. I fed the dogs, packed up my tools, my books, and my guitar and closed the door on the splintery little cabin that had been my home through four seasons in the Colorado Rockies, the place where I had planned to get away from it all. Wooly, Zoom, and I headed up to the café to say goodbye. Georgia was there. She wanted to go back to California, too.

— THE END —

The earth remains jagged and broken only to him or her who remains jagged and broken.

— Walt Whitman, *A Song of the Rolling Earth*

More books from Harvard Square Editions:

Dark Lady of Hollywood, Diane Haithman
Gates of Eden, Charles Degelman
Growing Up White, James P. Stobaugh
Sazzae, JL Morin
Calling the Dead, R.K. Marfurt
Close, Erika Raskin
Living Treasures, Yang Huang

CPSIA information can be obtained at www.ICGtesting.com
Printed in the USA
LVOW10s2134041115

461187LV00003B/113/P